SPACEHIVE

SPACEHIVE

Kenna McKinnon

Praise for SPACEHIVE

"SPACEHIVE is a fast paced, cross-pollination of a plot populated with invading giant wasps and bees sure to sting the imagination of its target audience." —Paula Shene, author of *Mandy the Alpha Dog*

"Sometimes humorous, sometimes terrifying, and always imaginative, this high-tech, interplanetary tale will keep you buzzing through page after page. You will never look at bees the same way!" —Val Muller, author of *Corgi Capers: Deceit on Dorset Drive*

"Wickedly funny and brimming with satire—a strange and quirky twist on the science fiction genre that will leave you in stitches. Highly recommended for youngsters and their parents alike!" —Derrick Hibbard, author of *Impish*

"Many novels have a sting in the tail, SPACEHIVE is literally full of them! I thoroughly enjoyed it from start to finish. SPACEHIVE is not only imaginative, but also extremely thought provoking. An absolute credit to this first time author. Bravo!" — Philip Parry, author of *Wishful Thinking*

"Don't get stung and miss this. You'll hive a great read and get a buzz." —Alan Place, author of *Pat Canella: The Dockland Murders*

With love to my children, Diane, Steven, Ward and my three grandsons.

Acknowledgements

Judith Hansen is a friend and editor who has thoughtfully and intelligently helped with this book. I also thank my publisher, Cheryl Tardif of Imajin Books, for her suggestions and patience. Without Judi's and Cheryl's professionalism and skill the book would not be the finished product it is.

My daughter Diane was a source of encouragement, support and help with the promotion of this book. I would like to thank my father, Kenneth Ross MacDonald, who loved science fiction, history and was my inspiration. I would also like to thank my mother, Patricia Jean MacDonald, who wrote as well. She and my father passed along their love of reading and writing to me, and the rest of my family has encouraged and shared my love of literature.

Phil Parry and his son Lee kindly read the manuscript before it was submitted and I'm grateful for their comments.

Prologue

Earth was in danger.

Jealous eyes gazed toward our Sun from a planet called Jive Hive in another star system, black compound eyes that peered without compassion as though we were flies caught on sticky paper ready for the fire.

The first of their suns was setting as blood-orange light spilled into the valley. Three female worker bees, two over seven feet tall and the other not quite five feet, sat under a purple-flowered tree, sorting through various blossoms, while other bees worked nearby.

"We can't go on like this much longer," Banter said. "There are too many of us. The hive has to find a new home. The Black Watch wasps, vicious as they are, know what they're doing. They've been scanning the skies for hundreds of years and keeping a check on our population."

She sat next to her cousins, Zibb and Bipp. They had worked all day collecting pollen for their hive. Now they rested and talked of the Imperative—to colonize. The whole Jive Hive planet was abuzz with the news.

"Yes," Zibb agreed. "The queen said this one is a plum ripe for the picking and only eight light years away. We'll be tired from the long sleep when we arrive. It'll be a brand new adventure for us. A new Jive Hive."

"Too bad there are beings there." Banter selected a fresh flower and began culling its nectar.

"Too bad we have to kill them all," Zibb said. "I've heard the new planet's green and warm. The wasp scouts said that it's abused by its inhabitants, though."

"Their fault then and all the more reason to kill them. We must take it while we can."

Zibb began grooming her cousin. "The migration will be an adventure to be endured before it's ended. They say the trip will take eight years in suspended animation. Then, on arrival, our poor, wasted bodies must prepare for war." She sighed.

"Or negotiation," Banter offered. She picked up another flower.

"Negotiation with General Vard and his black wasps? Never!" Zibb shook her barbs in the air. "The Black Watch wouldn't allow it. No, SpaceHive will deliver some of us to an early death once we've arrived on Earth. The humans are said to be a warlike race. I don't think they'll offer to share their planet. And our Black Watch sure won't share it. Earth will be taken by force and the human survivors used for food for the wasps."

Banter frowned. "I'll be sad, Zibb, to leave this haven of flowers, honey and sparkling waters."

"Me too. But it isn't a haven for many of our friends to the west, east and north. They're too crowded. Not enough to eat. Not like us, living close to the palace."

"Living close to our queen Selera. And she, poor dear, is old and sluggish, and listens too much to that horrible wasp, General Vard."

"The general says a new queen must travel with us to guide and reign over our species on the new soil." Zibb glanced at her smaller cousin Bipp. "Well, our old queen's endurance has seen her through the challenges of many rival daughter queens so far, lying now in tombs of wax with the queen's spike driven through their bodies."

To prepare the way, the royal jelly, culled from the milk glands of the nurse bees, would now be fed to the larva, who would then become a new queen.

The nurses often entertained the junior worker bees with a ditty.

Bzzzzz...ZAP! Honor the queen.
Bzzzzz...wake the hungry general.
Bzzzzz...he's black and full of poison.
Bzzzzz...ZAP! Hear us scream.

The song made everyone uneasy but was a source of amusement to the old nurses. There were other verses too. The bees loved song and dance.

Young Bipp brushed her fuzzy body with a barbed digit. "How will we know when we're leaving?"

"We won't, until the general tells us," Zibb said.

Bipp sighed. "Why can't we dance like we used to?"

"We all love to dance." Banter glanced at the hills where the Black Watch lived. "But there's more serious business now, little Cousin. We'll dance like nobody's going to die. But it won't be the joyful experience it always was for us."

"What? Killing the people of Earth so we might populate their planet?" Bipp drummed her digits on her bulging yellow abdomen. "That seems like a happy occasion to the general."

The bees had populated all the available planets in the star system, which lay on the edge of what Earth knew as the Milky Way. Now the Imperative rang out—*colonize or perish in your own numbers and material wealth.*

"The people of the green planet Earth will die," Banter said. "Nothing can save them. We have the war machine, SpaceHive and the deadly general. But some of us will die too, Bipp."

Banter stamped her foot and burst into an ancient nursery rhyme. "Bzzzzz...zap! Honor the old queen. Bzzzzz...zap! Long live the new!"

Bipp shook the gourds while Zibb played a fiddle fashioned from hard red wood and animal gut. Their old father drones built the fires. Their cousins and friends drummed on barrels and animal hides. All danced, whirled, flew and sang in high voices of ancient legends and science.

A drone huddled near a fire. "What legends are those you sing of?"

"Black poison and old science made new." Zibb stirred the flames as she pursed the black slit of her mouth. "General Vard doesn't approve of our emotional songs. But the old queen listens."

"Ah, the general." The drone cast a frightened glance up at the three orange moons. "Is that a shadow I see wheeling past the crescent of a moon?"

"No, it's nothing," Zibb said.

"I'm superstitious," the drone said, "though I don't believe in a god."

"What do you believe?"

"I believe in the necessity of the Black Watch and SpaceHive. I believe my body will rot in the general's larder if I disobey."

"The general calls this 'Ground Hundred,'" Zibb said. "I wonder what he means by that."

Banter played with a dark blossom. "He's been listening to old radio broadcasts from Earth."

"We don't have anything to say about the move." The drone turned away. "It's a military operation."

Migration to Earth was now a fact, issued directly from the queen, who got it from the general.

Standing over seven feet tall and winged, Zibb was an intelligent being, soft, pleasantly rounded and covered with orange fuzz. She had a pretty face dominated by huge black compound

4

eyes, small ears, mouth and antennae, which she was cleaning. She used the necessary hygiene as an excuse to rest and ponder. The Imperative was something new to think about.

"The first moon's going down," Bipp observed. "Let's build up the fire, Cousin Zibb. Like we always do. I don't want to dance and sing anymore. But let's huddle closer with our family and friends."

At first the Jive Hive had been ripe with nectar, pollen, fruit, trees and flowers. Rivers and brooks cascaded from springs high in the mountains. Now most of the planet's wealth was depleted. The rivers and brooks had dried up and nothing grew in the barren wastelands. No enemies existed except the pressure of population itself.

"We're lucky to live near the palace." Zibb crumpled the flower and threw it to the ground. "If Queen Selera weren't in our area and the general any farther away, we'd be starving too."

"Yes," Banter said. "They only allow us to gather the abundance and take what they don't want."

"But there's lots here for all of us," Bipp objected. "Why must we leave?"

"You don't understand, little Cousin. You haven't lived long enough to know about the other side of Jive Hive. The side where the wasps kill for a piece of rotting fruit. Thousands in less abundant areas are beginning to starve."

"Well, we'd give food to them."

"Not if you were starving. There are bloated bees all over the deserts of the west. Bees that have to compete to eat and drink." Zibb began to hum. "We're lucky here. The queen's closeness protects us. We're the special keepers of the palace. And the others? They don't come around here very often. They'd be spiked to death if they did, because we don't have room for them, Bipp."

"I see," Bipp said.

"The queen knows the Black Watch guards SpaceHive, a ship so powerful and huge it can carry half a planet through space to our new home, and bring us safely to foreign soil. We need the Black Watch wasps. *And* their technology. They're more than warriors—they're engineers and pilots."

Bipp's eyes widened.

"Nothing will defeat us," Zibb hissed. "We'll take them by surprise. Earth is doomed."

"Yes," a nurse matriarch spoke up. "They won't know what happened. We'll destroy them so fast. From deep space and their own fields and valleys, we'll sting them to death. We'll burn them."

Bipp laughed. "We have the machines."

"We have the wasps," Zibb said. "Black and frightful, they loom over us like giants. The Eternity Drive still exists from old times, hidden in the Hollow Hills near the Black Watch and guarded by the sergeants-at-arms. Their body fuzz is tipped with poison and their spikes are instant and deadly." She finished cleaning her antennae and turned to Banter, who was snoring by the fire. "Yes, the humans don't stand a chance."

The second of the orange moons set. Putrid light dripped like blood onto the valley.

Chapter One

As the wasps planned their invasion of Earth, Jason Anderson, a four-year-old boy from southwestern Canada, was stung by a small honeybee. He didn't feel a thing. He watched as the bee landed on his hand and the stinger went into his skin. Then the bee flew away.

"Jay!" his friend Buddy Ainsworth yelped. "You got stung."

"Don't feel nuffin'." Jason looked at his hand. There was no bump. The skin was smooth and fair.

Buddy frowned. "Aw, doesn't it hurt?"

"No."

Buddy ran to the big white house where Jason's mother stood at the window. "Mrs. Em! Jay got stung by a bee."

Emily Anderson ran down the wide stone steps. "Let me see. Is it swollen?"

He stuck out his unmarked hand.

"You're sure you were stung?"

"Yeah."

"He got bit all right, Mrs. Em." Buddy jumped from one foot to the other. "A bee got him. We were picking flowers."

"How many times must I tell you boys? Don't pick Greta's flowers next door. She loves her garden."

"Loves it like I love our cat Kitty-Winks?" her son asked.

His mother smiled. "Not quite that much."

"So how come I don't feel the bee sting?"

"I don't know, honey. We'll ask your father about this. He's very smart. You must be immune to bee stings."

At Buddy's confused look, Jason said, "Immune means we don't hurt when something bites us."

His mother nodded. "Lucky boy. I don't know where you got your immunity from. My arm swells when I get stung. I don't dare go near a bee."

Buddy slapped at a mosquito. The spot on which the insect had landed was already turning red. "Wish I was immune."

"If you were," Jason said, "then that mosquito wouldn't have hurt you, and your hand wouldn't have that red spot where he bit you."

"He sucked my blood," Buddy declared. He glanced up at Mrs. Anderson. "Is Jay's dad a doctor?"

"Not a medical doctor, Bud. He's a PhD, a Doctor of Philosophy. He's a biochemist."

"Oh. A bee-chemistry guy." Buddy laughed at his own joke.

"He does research on natural chemicals. Jason here is going to be a biochemist too. Aren't you, honey?"

He gave a nod.

"Why do you want to do that?" Buddy asked his friend.

Jason shrugged. "It's cool."

"He's very interested in bees and other insects," his mother replied. She put her arms around both the boys and led them up the stone steps. "Apple juice and brownies, anyone?"

The robotess they had bought for a tutor wheeled along behind them, holding flowers in a cup. Jason glanced back at her. He loved his new robot teacher. She taught him about beauty and truth.

"The bee didn't hurt me," he mumbled. "I'm immune to bee stings."

Garter snakes wiggled through the tall grass in old Greta's garden. No way Jason would go there again. He hated snakes, but bees were okay.

The brownies and apple juice were delicious. Kitty-Winks, his small grey cat, curled around the robotess's silver feet, and Buddy shared green Gummigators from a bag in his pocket.

By the time his father returned home from work, Jason had forgotten all about the bee sting. In fact, he didn't remember it until eight years later—when alien bees invaded Earth.

Chapter Two

On planet Jive Hive, General Vard's vicious Black Watch wasp soldiers lived in papery wasp hives under the cliffs of the Hollow Hills. They guarded the spy devices that searched the sky every night and the huge ship—SpaceHive.

Each soldier was over nine feet tall and wore a black patch so he could be identified as part of the evil general's special force. Fierce and cold-hearted, they would fight to the death.

"Attention," one of the wasp soldiers announced as the general made his way toward them.

General Vard's barbed arms scraped together. "We go to the valley tonight to tell my plan to the workers and drones. I will go to the queen to talk about matters of state."

"Matters of state?" A young sergeant snapped to attention. "Are the rumours true then, sir? Are we going to have a new queen?"

"None of your beeswax, soldier."

With one swift motion, the general stabbed the young wasp in the neck. His friends ate the fallen sergeant right away.

"That's better," the general said to a slim wasp standing beside him. "Now clean up this mess, Captain Pecula, and report to me first thing tomorrow morning. I want all the soldiers on full parade by noon tomorrow. We must make a show of force to impress those lazy, good-for-nothing workers and drones. And tell them to shape up so they can ship out when I say so, with no whining from even the smallest of them."

"I'm sure they'll be just fine, sir," the captain said. "The death rays and weapons are ready. We have the maps and graphs we need, and the pilots can hardly wait to take off."

"Remember now, we must not destroy the planet Earth. Just the people. We want to be able to live on the planet after the humans are dead." He scratched his chin. "If the humans give up and don't fight, kill them all for food. If they fight, they fight to the death anyway."

"What happens when Earth is crowded like our home, the Jive Hive?" Captain Pecula asked. "When there are too many new queens, new workers and drones, what then?"

"Then we move on. But that is light years away."

"We can't expand forever."

The general gave him a hard look and the captain closed his mouth. "We can and we will, Captain Pecula."

"I won't ask any more questions, sir."

"That's smart." The general grunted. "Now I must meet with Queen Selera. I must convince her she can't come with us to our new home. She must feed a younger queen, one who will lead us into victory in this new world."

"Yes, sir."

"A couple of centuries from now," the general mused, "another general will decide the fate of Earth when there will be too many of us again. He'll take his decision to a future queen, who will give orders to seek out a new home."

A lieutenant looked at the poisoned tip of the general's spike. "We'll have to limit our population another way after we've used up Earth. The Eternity Drive can't take us any farther..."

Anger gleamed in the general's eyes. *"Who else knows how the War Games are going to end?" He held the lieutenant up with his stubby barbed hands.*

"Only five of us know." The lieutenant gasped. *"Besides me, all majors."*

"I'll talk to them." The general let the soldier fall to the ground. *"Perhaps they can be trusted. But they must be questioned. Captain Pecula?"*

"Yes, sir, I'll bring them right away."

"I'll see the queen first."

The general flew into the night, down the valley, up the slopes to the royal palace. His grim figure was a fearful shadow against the second of the setting three moons.

"You don't have enough honey in your system, General Vard," the old bee queen said and heaved her body to a more comfortable position. "Do the War Games really say our migrations will end?"

"This move may be the last migration to another planet. After that. . . " The general flexed his spiky black hands, rattled his sword.

"Mercy killing of any bees who can't find food on the earth at that time," the queen finished. "We'll need more land in a century or two, and Earth is our last hope. We've moved to all the other known planets in the star systems we can get to. After Earth has been used up, perhaps we could kill our own bees with a virus and they won't know where it came from. We'd have to make room for the rest of us. Who else knows of this matter?" The queen's shoulders rippled.

"Four senior officers, along with Captain Pecula, you and I."

"Five too many soldiers. Kill them."

"Yes, Highness." The general grinned. "Orders have already been given."

"And the workers and drones you're shipping to Earth?"

"They'll be happy once again, under the vigilant eyes of my Black Watch. We'll be happy for a long time, after we've killed the humans."

"For a hundred years or more, I think," the queen said. "I've bought them that much time."

"Now," the general rasped. "Prepare the new queen. She must be warlike. And strong."

"I will see to it."

The general saluted. "Your majesty." General Vard flew off, after a stiff bow to Her Royal Highness.

The workers and drones in the valley below huddled closer as they saw the dread image cross over the third moon up to the paper caverns hidden in the Hollow Hills.

"A new young queen will be chosen by the old queen from the dozens of female eggs she lays every day," the general explained to his soldiers. "The new queen will be beautiful and grow to be wise. She'll be healthy, fit and full of life. She'll be spared, fed with royal jelly and grow to be a queen in her own right—smart and warlike enough to guide our bees to their new world."

Yes, a new queen would lead them into war, under the eye of the Black Watch. So it would be. A young and strong queen. The old queen would stay on the old Jive Hive and watch over a failing population.

The wasps were happy.

Chapter Three

"Only the Black Watch knows when we leave," Zibb said to her cousins that night at the dance, where they whirled to the Music of the Wings. The dances had become places of heated discussion and fights.

"Only legends exist of other homes." It was the old nurse from the palace. The nurses loved to gossip. "A young queen lies asleep in wax, fed royal jelly. The old queen grows sluggish. Her egg sacs are drying up. Soon she'll retire."

"What will we do?" Bipp asked.

"The general wants half our planet of workers to go, nurses and a few drones necessary to tend the new queen, and the Black Watch in charge. The other bees and some wasps will remain on our world."

The workers were upset. They didn't want to be separated from their friends and family. "When do we leave?" Bipp's small mouth shook.

"Soon," Zibb said, stirring the fire while the nurses and drones huddled together. "Very soon."

"Those who are chosen by the general will go. Those who are chosen by the old queen will go too. We'll sleep in the spaceship on the way to a new home. We'll awake in eight years." The nurse would not go on the trip. She was too old.

There wasn't much time to prepare. The best time to leave was now, when their Jive Hive swung close to Earth.

Then the day of migration came.

"General Vard is walking among the workers and drones," Banter said. She and Zibb were lined up with thousands of others to enter the spaceship, which they called the SpaceHive. "I don't like it."

"He's a danger to all of us," Zibb agreed. "But we're born with the physical necessity to obey our Queen and then her guards."

SpaceHive was the size of a small continent. Buzzing with excitement, the workers and drones filed on board. They took their places in soft wax-carved rooms.

The bees took a deep breath before the Black Watch gave them something to make them sleep, adjusted the needles for a constant drip of honey in their veins and sealed them in. The nurses were the last to be put under. The old nurses were not there.

"I want everything tight and secure, soldiers," the general said. "Check the battle armour again, and the war weapons stored on board. Check the war machines, the smaller skyships in the hold and the battle plans. I want nothing to go wrong at the end of our trip. Kill the humans! Populate Earth. Let's go."

The general waved his sword. He handed a lance to a sergeant. All hand weapons were coated with poison.

"We have a lot of weapons to defend our new queen and take over a new planet. The humans won't be a match for our deadly heat guns, our death rays and war machines. We'll take over this new planet or we'll die."

The sergeant rattled his barbs and waved the poison lance in the air.

"We must now put ourselves into the hands of the automatic pilots," the general said. "Seal up Queen Taranta and ourselves.

We have extra eggs just in case something happens to our dear new queen."

So the huge ship SpaceHive shot through space at the speed of light, its cargo of bees, wasps and eggs sleeping, dreaming in wax rooms.

The passengers from Jive Hive woke eight years later, their faces stuffed with wax, tubes of honey and nectar still dripping into their bodies. The automatic pilot screamed to a halt at the solar system on the rim of the Milky Way. General Vard took over the controls.

Zibb and Banter rubbed their eyes. Zibb looked around for her other cousins. Some still slept in their rooms. "Where's Bipp?" Zibb asked.

"I don't know if we all made it." Banter yawned.

The new queen took her place by the general's side.

"Our gentle cousin *has* to live." Zibb left and began to look for Bipp throughout the ship. She returned to Banter's side. "I couldn't find her," Zibb said.

"We're all hungry. She may have wandered off in search of more honey after the machines woke her up," Banter said between sips of liquid honey from a feeding tube. "Or the general may have become hungry and..." She didn't want to finish the thought.

Zibb struck her fuzzy forehead with a claw. "I know where the curious Bipp would be! In the viewing room looking at the lights of the universe. She would be relieving herself on the way back in one of the portapoops."

"Of course. She's a clever little bee and like you say, Zibb, curious. No harm will come to Bipp. She's much loved even by the Black Watch."

Just then Bipp emerged from a room down a long corridor, alive and humming.

"Bipp," Zibb said, "you're a bad young bee to worry your cousin so."

"Are we there yet, Cousin Zibb?"

"Yes, dear. Almost there."

"Can I meet a human?" Bipp was indeed a curious little bee.

"Sure. There are lots of them to slaughter," Zibb said.

"I guess we'll get there secretly?"

"Probably. I think that's the plan." Zibb looked at Banter, who put down the feeding tube. Banter's black mouth slit curved up when she looked at Bipp.

"Oh, I love surprises." Bipp smacked four of her digits together. "Maybe I can talk to one before I have to kill it?"

"I wouldn't be surprised, dear," Zibb agreed.

The ship hovered above Earth. It followed a wave of electronic noise to the North American continent, then SpaceHive landed in a quiet place in the mountains of southern British Columbia. The wasps sent the smaller spaceships and their weapons to hover over the rest of Earth. All had the same message for Earth.

"Turn on the master translator." General Vard took his place on the bridge. Spit dripped from the general's jaws. He was enjoying this.

"Now hear this." The translators boomed through all electronic speakers on Earth. "Now hear this. We come in peace."

From the hives and fields of Earth, billions of bumble bees, killer bees, honeybees, hornets and wasps flew to the ships. Any human in their path was stung to death.

"More later," the general boomed to the men and women of Earth. The skyships roared into place on every part of the globe. The humans had no weapons strong enough to defend themselves against the mighty war machines.

The alien bees claimed a new Jive Hive.

Chapter Four

The alien bees and wasps were quiet for two days. Their new home lay blue and green beneath the great ship, SpaceHive. Their new Queen Taranta, a huge bee, stood beside General Vard and looked below. "It's beautiful. We could do a lot with it. You've done well, General."

The wasp general sat in front of the translator and buzzed his warning in words that everyone on Earth could understand. His words rang through all the earth.

"Surrender or die! We give you no choice, people of Earth. I know you understand me. Lay down your weapons. We have the war machines, the Black Watch, the death rays. We'll blast you with death from our ships. As well, our small cousins in the fields and hills of Earth are now on board. More are coming. Your beekeepers would do well to stay out of their way. We are your future. We come in peace."

He grinned and smacked his palms together. The bees laughed.

"What should we do, sir?" the minister of staff asked the prime minister of Canada.

"Call the president," the prime minister said. "Call the United Federation of Nations and our European allies. Call Russia,

China and India. We must agree to work together. We've never faced a danger like this before."

And the earth's leaders gathered to devise a strategy.

"There'll be no going back," the wasp general said when he heard the earth leaders' decision. "There'll be no mercy. Small ships are now flying over your planet, over all countries and nations." His voice boomed over Earth in all languages.

"We're at war with an alien species," the chairperson of the world congress said to the head of the nations of the world, an organization called the United Federation of Nations, or UFN.

"Our information says the local honeybees, small bumblebees and hornets in the fields and forests of Earth have swarmed to the ship on top of the Purcell Mountains in British Columbia." The chairperson turned to the prime minister of Canada who sat in a meeting with his chief of staff.

"But they're not the danger. Seven-foot-tall alien bees and nine-foot-tall wasps have come out of the ship. They brought the huge war machine as a threat. I'm afraid they'll use it any minute."

The prime minister looked to the other heads of nations around the table. The king of Jordan cleared his throat. "We'll contain them. Bring out our weapons of mass destruction. This is the time for them."

Meanwhile, the war machines rained death from the mountains and skies of Earth. Humans heard the thunder and buzz of billions of huge aliens in pods and airships all over the earth. It seemed the alien bees could not fly in the higher gravity of Earth, but they didn't have to fly because they had the machines.

"Tell us what to do!" screamed the inhabitants of Earth to their leaders. They were met with confused silence. "Our military is helpless against the shields of the mother ship and the rays of the death machines," the generals of Earth said.

Five Star Earth General Joseph Zellers, the Chief of Defense at the UFN, snorted. "Bomb them! We have weapons of mass destruction. It's time to use them."

"What weapons of mass destruction?" a sheikh asked. "We have camels and oil, olive groves and Allah on our side."

"We have no choice but to bomb them," the Australians said.

"No, we don't dare use nuclear weapons," said the Canadian Prime Minister. "They'd be suicide for the people of Earth."

"We'll nuke the gravy out of them." General Zellers folded his hands over his big belly and winked at President Maria Black.

"I'm with you, Joseph. Time's not on our side."

"Their armour, sabres and spikes are mainly for show," the social scientists on Earth said. "Their Black Watch has awesome high-tech machines like the death rays and war machines which poke from openings in the SpaceHive and their other ships. We're unable to blast through their shields. But we'll find a way. We'll knock them off the Purcell Mountains. We'll call out all experts on bees and their kind."

"Nuke them," General Zellers shouted.

When it was apparent that Earth would fight back, the huge alien species shut themselves in their SpaceHive and airships, some on the ground and some in the air. The death rays blazed and smoked from their war machines. Humanity and Earth were seared, and crisp black deserts appeared in the green valleys of Earth. The air was thick with the smell of burning flesh.

Marines were sent to attack the ships on the ground. The fighter jets fired on them without success. Local people built underground rooms to protect the children, the elderly and the sick.

The UFN met on a daily basis. There were arguments and they were slow to act. The chairperson resigned. Military rule was declared.

"Earth will never surrender," General Zellers of the UFN said.

"We weren't given the chance," the peacemakers replied. "They won't let us surrender."

"We'll never surrender," millions of people of all nations agreed.

They rose up from the grassroots to attack the aliens. The rest went underground, to homes hidden in caves and under oceans.

Many were trapped in their high-tech cars and air scooters. No one but General Zellers and President Black dared think of using nuclear weapons.

"The people of Earth must be united to fight the invaders," President Black declared. "They are terrorists. Attack!" Prisons were emptied so the prisoners could go to war. Men and women were given guns and sent to fight.

"We're sending out our best fighter planes and bombers with missiles and deadly pesticides," Zellers said. "But nothing can get through the enemy's shields. Their war machines and death rays burn us alive."

The president rubbed her forehead in contemplation. "All our best people are being hired in the war effort. Find a pesticide, a disease, to destroy the wasps. Find a way to cure the venom that kills us. Put poison in their food supply. Destroy their ships. Their translators use fear to bring us to our knees. We won't be bullied. Mankind will win."

Money was printed in large amounts to support the war effort. Stock markets all over Earth collapsed. People bought war bonds which became pieces of worthless paper when nations fell. India and China at first remained strong. Finally they too fell to the attacks and wasp swarms that came from the air and their own fields and forests.

China kept secrets. People said they were building starships to escape Earth. Rumour only. The rest of the world was without hope but kept fighting.

"Ordinary warfare is useless. The ship they call SpaceHive and their smaller airships are safe behind their shields and guns."

The prime minister of Canada visited the western provinces and promised help.

"We'll put our best minds to work. We'll fight to the finish."

Bunkers were poured in concrete under the ground. General Zellers and the UFN again talked about a nuclear attack. Their partners agreed a nuclear attack might destroy the earth.

So the bitter, fiery months passed.

Jason's father knew the answer to mankind's survival must lie in science. A treatment must be found to cure the victims and a poison must be found that would destroy the aliens.

"I'll do what I can," Stephen said when his bosses ordered him to the war effort. "My lab is safe in the forests of Yahk near the mother ship. And we're working on something that might help."

"Nuke them!" another high ranking Earth officer said. "They're killing us all!"

"Give us time," a scientist said. "Nuclear weapons could kill us all, including the earth itself."

"We don't have time," a soldier replied. "Our people are dying by the millions."

"We need a weapon that will attack the way their bodies work. A chemical," a politician replied. "We need Professor Anderson and others like him. Wait. Give us time."

Chapter Five

Twelve-year-old Jason tossed his long red hair on a wrinkled pillow and moaned in his sleep. He was having a bad dream. Boa constrictors were twisting from the sheets to squeeze his chest. He'd been playing Guitar Mozart the night before and had eaten a lot of salted chips. He'd washed them down with Purple Pony sports drink.

The chips and drink might have given him bad dreams, but more likely it was the talk he'd had with his parents just before going to bed. He moaned again. He hated snakes. He felt smothered by the snakes and smothered by his parents. Odd he hadn't dreamed of the bees and wasps. But Jason was different than most boys, with faith in science to protect Earth.

"Go away." He opened his green eyes. "You're choking me. Go away!"

Lights burned from the LCD display on his ceiling.

"Jay?" His mother stood by the door with her hand on the light port.

"I'm all right. Go back to bed, Mom. It was just a bad dream." He closed his eyes again.

"You know my work keeps me away from home a lot," his father had told him earlier that day. His father was a biochemist.

He had put an arm around his son's shoulders, but Jason inched away. He was downloading music into his new personal audio device (PAD). He placed the ZipPAD on the kitchen table.

His mother picked up the electronic tablet.

"I'm not finished, Mom."

His mother smiled. "We had one like this in Library Technology at college. Mine was old compared to this one, Jay."

"Try it. You can download music from the computer tablet on the wall."

His father cleared his throat and scratched the reddish-blond whiskers on his chin. "I've been counting on you, Jay, to look after your mother while I'm in the lab in Yahk. Here in Creston we're on our own, left pretty much alone to deal with the threat from the aliens."

"I know that, Dad. We're at the end of the world far as anyone knows. What do your bosses say in the east, Dad?"

"The head office expects me to do my research by myself, only checking in with Cranbrook once a day and Ottawa every week. We're pretty safe here, though we're close to the mother ship. However, the bees pick on bigger cities and towns. But this is my plan—"

"It's the government's plan." Jason brushed off the shoulder that his father had touched. "They don't want your research public, Dad. They want to learn how to fight a war with chemicals. I'm not stupid. I can help."

"I know you're not stupid, Jay. You're a very bright young man. My research would be used for a strike against the wasps before they knew what hit them. They won't be expecting it. Our federal government needs me. And they need boys like you—ones who are good at science and math—to grow up and take my place."

"Is that what you want to talk to me about?"

"No, that's not what we want to talk to you about tonight. You've already guessed it."

"I know." He moved a little farther away. His mother pinched her lips, smoothing the Betty Boop apron she wore, which showed the little bulge around her waist. She finished downloading Brahms's Third Symphony into Jason's ZipPAD as well as the latest audio from a hockey game he had enjoyed.

"I know you'll love your music and books when you're away from home," she said. "Jay, keep up your lessons. Keep up your interest in your father's research. Enjoy your music and languages. Uber-new is fine, uber-new is good, but learn some of the old retro stuff too, son. You'll be teaching the smaller one someday. You'll be a fine big brother."

"I don't *want* a new little brother or sister. That's what you want to talk about?"

His father folded his hands into a steeple and his mother frowned.

"No, Jay, it's more than that," his father said. "Our government needs us. We face a danger only guessed at by the general public. A danger never faced before. Soon we won't be able to keep it secret. The families of federal workers are being sent to underground rooms in Kamloops until the war is over."

"Am I going, Dad? And Mom and Kitty-Winks?"

"Your mother, Kitty-Winks and the robotess are going there soon. You've heard how some of your friends are missing. Some are in the bunkers already with their families and some have been... well, they've come too close to the death rays and the wasps."

"More secrets?"

"We're all part of the war effort, Jay."

"What are you trying to tell me, Dad? That I'll be sent away too, like Mom?"

"I know you don't want to go. We knew you'd say that. I'm telling you—"

"No, I'll stay and fight. My friend Buddy is dead and I haven't seen Grayson for weeks. My other friends are already in underground bunkers in Kamloops. I want to learn about the war here and how I can help."

"Jay, listen to me."

"My friends didn't have time to fight back. Now I'll pay back the wasps for Buddy, Grayson and more who died in the first wave of invaders."

"No more secrets, Jay. You'll help with the war effort. You'll stay with me."

He nodded. "I'll miss you, Mom. Maybe you can do some library work there in the bunkers? That's what you're trained for. Your files are already there in the computer. You can maybe work alone, keep in touch by PAD. Protect my baby brother and help save the world."

"Yes. I can help with the research from the tablets in the bunkers. Your father and I have talked about how I can help. And you, Jay, I'm very proud of you. You can help, too."

"Yeah. By giving blood that's immune to bee venom. And keeping out of the way."

"Jay."

"Just you wait and see. Just you wait."

Jason's nose was running. He wiped a dirty fist across his face and ran into the next room. He already missed his friends.

He was frightened, but he would face his fears and win.

In the living room, Stephen paced the floor. "I'm still fairly young, Emily, with a PhD in chemistry and biology, and a special interest in bees and wasps. Perfect job to fight the aliens. I'm a scientist. A good one. Blood tests taken after the aliens got here have shown that Jay has genes that could produce an antidote and a weapon that would attack their blood. I need him with me. I'm sorry."

Emily patted his arm. "I know, Steve. I know our family has to be separated."

"You know what they say about honor, love and war. This is a war unlike any we've ever known. You'll have to move to the underground bunkers in Kamloops to be safe. Jason and I will stay in the lab in Yahk. I'll homeschool him like we've always done. I'll be able to concentrate on my work, knowing you're all safe."

"Are you responsible to your family or to the government, Steve? I can't leave you for that long, not knowing what will happen to you or how long it'll be before I see you and Jason again. If ever."

"I'm responsible to the world now." He tugged at the red-blond growth of hair on his chin. "Emily, you know how I feel about you and Jay and our unborn child. I never expected this when I signed up for government work. But we all have to do our part."

"That means sending me away?"

"I don't want to, but it's just too dangerous for you out here. And we have to think about the baby. Jay may be safer with me. I don't know. I do know we need him. We need to study his immunity."

"Yes, I know that. And the new baby has to be kept safe." She patted her belly.

Stephen frowned. "I don't know how Jay got his immunity, but it showed up as quite a small boy. The tests we do might be just what we need to solve this puzzle."

"But why can't I stay with you? If you can protect Jay, you can protect me too."

"You know that most families are either dead or have fled."

She nodded.

"And you know, Emily, there's nothing you can do here. Soon you won't be safe, even here where the bees and wasps appear to have forgotten us in the mountains. You're allergic to bee or wasp stings. You could die if you were stung by these aliens. And the baby. If the war machine opens up on us we'll die anyway."

"I'd be safe in the bunkers. You and Jay—"

"You and the baby will be safer in the underground bunkers in Kamloops. There are doctors there to look after the birth if you're in the bunkers that long. I can join you after my work's done. I promise, Em."

"We won't think of the chance of losing the war."

"No, we won't. We'll talk on a special channel on our Zip-PADs, you deep in the concrete bunkers with other wives and families waiting out the war."

If an end to the war could be found.

"You and our son will be working alone, torn from your family and friends." Emily wiped her eyes and hugged her husband.

"We won't lose," he said. To lose would be to lose their unborn child and Jason too.

"It's the personal losses that people mourn, not the big losses of the whole world that we don't know about yet," Emily said. "I'm thinking of our children and you, Steve. Surely my library work would be useful?"

"It will. Your library files are essential. And you'll be doing that in the underground bunkers. We need your skills, Em. We need the baby, and we need you both alive. Promise you'll go?"

"Fine. I promise. Call me every day?"

"At ten in the morning and six at night."

Jason rose from the chair in the next room where he listened and padded to the kitchen door. His red hair blazed in the sun, which streamed through an open window.

His robotess didn't meet him at the kitchen door as it usually did. He missed the smooth metal touch of the robot already, the hum of its teaching voice, the security of its face.

His parents met him at the door.

"I'll come with you, Dad."

He took his books and lab equipment with him to his father's lab at Yahk and of course his ZipPAD which was loaded with new millennium rock, jazz, as well as the trendy older music of his parent's time and the Brahms music his mother uber-loaded.

Oddly, his parents knew all the new tunes, which were re-worked from an earlier era. Music had been doing that since the early twenty-first century, but that didn't bother Jason. He loved music of any kind—retro, post rap or Guitar Mozart.

"Or anything with a beat," he'd explained once to Grayson.

But Grayson had gone missing in the first wave of the wasp invasion. Then there was Buddy, his childhood friend. Jason didn't like to think of his friend burned to cinders in front of him.

"Buddy...Grayson." Jason clenched his fists.

"What's wrong?" his father asked.

"You just need me for your experiments, Dad. I'm tired of giving blood. I've filled out hundreds of pages of tests. Have you figured out the immunity from bee venom I've had since a kid? No, you haven't. You haven't saved a single life, though you say you have the serum put together. The answer lies in making a toxin from my blood that would kill the aliens. Now *that* would be awesome. But meantime they're killing us all."

"I want a serum that will help humanity, Jay. Your mother is busy putting together information, deep in the bunkers near Kamloops. Our whole family is part of the war effort. You're a hero, Jay."

He sighed and rolled up his sleeve again.

"I'm sorry Buddy and Grayson are gone," his father said. "I'm sorry your other friends are underground in bunkers and you can't talk to them through the channel your mother and I share. I'm sorry I can't be with you more. But this is more important work than anyone has ever done. It's to save Earth."

Chapter Six

"Victory's uncertain and humanity seems doomed to lose the war. We are scattered and mostly unable to act." Stephen's bosses in Cranbrook called him daily with the same basic message.

Jason didn't allow thoughts of defeat to enter his mind.

"Where are you going, Jay? Out to wander through the forest again?" His father peered into the bright computer images on the wall and made some changes to the formula. "Be careful, Son."

"Yeah. Careful is as careful does." He twisted his thumb on the volume and popped his ZipPAD into a pocket of his summer jacket. He hummed as he went out the door.

He missed his friends and wondered if a brother would be born. His parents hadn't shared with him whether the new baby would be a boy or girl.

"Do you know, Dad? Is it going to be a boy? You and Mom maybe chose not to know. Jeepers. *Everyone* now knows the gender of an unborn child."

His father said nothing. He was busy with an experiment. Liquid bubbled in a test tube over a small burner.

"My parents are very antique if not unique." He hoped to get a rise out of his father. "I wouldn't put it past you not to know. It's going to be a brother, you know. Stephen Canada Anderson Jr."

"You know that, do you, Jay?"

"Yeah, Dad. See you later, alligator."

He began to do his school work in the mornings and went out later in the day. He explored the area around the lab. A path sliced through another property.

"There's a house across the road," he muttered to himself. Then, "Oh hi, you mutt!"

A grey terrier wagged his rear end and smiled in a doggy way. Muddy paws smeared his jeans.

"My dog bothering you?" A bearded, stooped man bent to avoid a branch, grabbed the small dog by his collar and pulled him off Jason. "He don't mean no harm. Been hunting rats in the rock pile out back."

"A dog that hunts rats?" He didn't know much about dogs. His parents were cat people. Kitty-Winks was in the bunker with his mother and the robotess. Jason missed his pet.

"Yeah. He's a cairn terrier. Born and bred in him to hunt rats."

"That's cool. What's its name?"

"Freedom. And I'm Bill Glass. Live in that old shed over there." The man gestured with his left hand, the right holding a chain fastened to Freedom's collar. A small pine grew from the shed's moss roof. The door sagged open and one window was boarded up.

Jason raised a brow. *Our lab is a palace compared to that shack.* He began to feel sorry for the man and his dog.

"That's a funny name for a dog," Jason said.

Mr. Glass chuckled. "After my divorce, I wanted freedom, so I got this mutt."

Jason laughed. He got the joke, even though he was a kid. Some of his friends were children of divorce. "Freedom. Exactly what we need now."

Mr. Glass nodded, his expression now serious. "I agree."

31

Jason knew Mr. Glass was harmless. His mother often brought the man fresh bread. They often saw him weeding his garden or walking Freedom.

"They've chosen names for my brother," he said to Mr. Glass later. "If it's a boy, Stephen Canada Anderson Jr., and if it's a girl, Victoria Emily, for victory and love. They either don't know I'm getting a brother, or they don't want to tell me. But it won't be a girl."

"We're all doomed," Mr. Glass said.

"Because I'm getting a sister?"

Mr. Glass shook his head. "Because of the alien invasion."

"We're not doomed. My dad is working on a cure. He already has some stuff made from my blood. It's the first step toward creating a poison that can fight against the aliens. I helped. It's my blood."

A couple of days later someone pounded on their door early in the morning. Jason followed his father down the stairs. They found Mr. Glass outside.

"Help me," the man said, gasping. "A swarm of small earth bees stung my dog almost to death."

"I think we can help," his father said. He disappeared for a second and when he returned he withdrew liquid from a test tube with a thick needle. "Here, Jay. You know what to do. It's time we tested the serum."

With the needle in hand, Jason ran outside. Near Mr. Glass's house, Freedom's body lay twitching and swollen.

"Here, Love." He plunged the needle deep into the dog's side. Nothing happened.

Then Freedom stopped twitching and opened his eyes. The dog got to his feet, shook himself and walked away.

"Look at that, would ya." Mr. Glass slapped Jason on the back. "Gosh, how'd you do that?"

"My dad did it. He made the serum."

"You saved my dog. Thank you."

"What've you done with the formula?" Jason said to his father that afternoon. "It works! It's not just stored in the safe for later, is it?"

"Still too soon to tell. We must get it right the first time. It worked on a dog. Will it work on humans? Will we be able to fight the aliens with it? It could be used for a lot of things—saving humans, saving animals, changed a bit and used for killing aliens with their own venom. But we have to be sure."

"Aw, Dad! By the time you and the feds are sure, we'll all be dead. We have to be fast. We have to take a risk and go for it."

"Jason, the formula still has to be created and the doses figured out for both humans and wasps if it's going to do what we want it to. It worked on a dog. Once. Maybe that was sheer chance."

"It will work. I know it will."

"We need something to make us well if we're poisoned by the aliens, and something that will kill the wasps from inside, turn their own venom against them. It's our only hope. Our weapons don't work on the airships or SpaceHive."

"We'll get them from inside, Dad. We'll surprise them."

"There's more of them and they're smarter than we are. They have better machines, better computers and shields on their airships that we can't get through."

"They have better machines, but they're not smarter than us. There's a way, and we've got to start with your serum. I know it."

Jason turned on his ZipPAD and thumbed a number.

"How's Freedom?" he asked. "Any side effects?"

"Freedom's fine." Mr. Glass said. "That stuff you gave him was awesome, Jason. A miracle."

Jason exchanged a few more words with the man, then disconnected the call. "See, Dad. The serum worked."

His father let out a tired sigh. "Now if only I can get it to work at curing and immunizing humans."

Jason nodded. *And kill those evil wasps.*

Chapter Seven

Jason's walks took him closer to the alien's skyship every time he went out. He spent more time outside and didn't do all his homework. His father didn't seem to notice. Mr. Glass and Freedom were the boy's only friends.

His father sent his data to the war effort in Ottawa and stayed out of the way of the bees and wasps—he searched the world for answers. He was skilled in multiple languages, including Russian, Chinese, Japanese and Hindustani. He read and wrote science papers in French. He knew Greek and Latin.

"I'll teach you everything I know, Jay. See this? It's Latin. *Cogito ergo sum.* I think, therefore I am."

Jason began to pick up words and phrases in other languages. He tried to understand the science his father worked on. Because of that, he aced his homeschooling, even though he spent more time outside. He still missed the robotess, and every morning at ten and evening at six they talked to Jay's mother.

His father returned from trips to Cranbrook to meet with his boss. He brought back treats—Jason's favorite candies.

"Green Gummigators! Thanks, Dad." He shared them with Freedom. "I'm not afraid to walk alone at night so close to the mother ship. I've studied the bees and wasps. Most of them sleep at night. Maybe I'll see a big one someday."

He tried to text on his ZipPAD to anyone who would talk to him. No one answered. His mother didn't answer, either, as it was past six o'clock. Jason swept his overgrown hair from his eyes. His buddies would've teased him for sure. He asked his father to cut his hair.

"Haircut, Jay? No, I'm too busy for that. Ask the neighbour, or cut it yourself. Anyhow, it looks pretty good like that. Sort of a wild-boy-Anderson look, red like mine. You got a nice mane of hair there."

Jason had just set his ZipPAD to voice mode. At a word, the personal audio device opened the front door of the lab to let in the cool night air while he waited for his father to finish his tests.

His father raised one eyebrow and peered into a vial of bubbling liquid. Numbers flashed on the wall computer. He squinted up at the figures and entered more numbers into his tablet.

Jason was positive his father was close to a cure.

Zibb often walked through the forests near Yahk at night when the other bees stayed inside their ship. She wasn't sleepy like they were after dark.

That night, she danced through the trees and tangled shrubs when only small creatures of the woods were out. The wind howled and the moon cast its ghostly glow as she passed by Jason's father's lab.

SpaceHive loomed ahead like a steel monster.

Zibb strode toward the front of the ship, heard music and her feet danced.

Jason picked up his summer jacket, put his feet into open retro sneakers and slipped his ZipPAD into a pocket. He went out into the silent misty night.

Music burst from his ZipPAD and he turned it up, bipping and bopping to the tune. He stopped, thinking he heard a noise on the path ahead. "Who are you?"

Jason hugged his jacket around his lean body and shivered. The night was cold. He thought maybe the aliens in the mother ship on the mountain could hear the song. He wondered what they would do. But he wasn't afraid. "Mr. Glass? Freedom?" he called. "Is that you? Who's out there?"

Cogito ergo sum. I think, therefore I am. He felt better as he thought about the words his father had taught him.

Science will save the earth. Moonlight and music have nothing to do with it. I'm just feeling funny because it's late, and I'm tired.

He ran a hand through his hair.

There's danger here if any of the aliens are out tonight.

Jason didn't think they would be awake, but who knew when it came to the bees? A dark cloud flew across the face of the moon, casting a purple shadow over the forest. He looked around and heard a noise like wings scraping together.

Someone sang a little song. Someone who didn't sound afraid.

"Bzzzz...Zat! Bzzzz...Zappa.

The general is near.

I am here.

Hear us scream!

Bzzzzzzzz...Zappa!"

A giant bee was chanting the song, holding a red translator in her hands. Her feet moved in time to the music and Jason stopped when he saw her. He kept his voice even. "Holy moly. A bee! You're not inside at night like the rest of your friends?"

He turned down the volume and slipped the PAD back in his pocket. "This is the first time I've seen one of you bees so close." Jason didn't know if the bee could understand him, but he'd heard about their science and knew the little red box could translate his words.

"I have nowhere to run and hide, no weapons." Jason spread his hands. "I'm immune to you and that protects me," he continued, hoping to talk long enough so he could find out something more about the aliens than was already known.

The music and Jason's voice seemed to calm the huge bee. She swayed and her feet moved. Jason moved toward the side of the road and put his hands in his pockets. He tried to dial his father on his PAD, jammed his thumbs against the controls, but the keys didn't respond. The speakers hissed with static.

"Don't hurt me," Jason said. His heart pounded beneath the thin jacket he wore. The wind blew through the trees beside the road.

"You are beautiful," the bee buzzed.

"What?"

She spoke into the red box held in her hands. "You're beautiful. Your red hair is streaked with silver moonlight."

She grabbed him. Jason fought back, but the alien was very strong. The bee held him close and began to dance back along the path toward the mother ship. He had no choice but to go along. Her strong barbed arms carried him toward the alien craft.

"Stop," Jason cried as they reached the ship. "You've made a mistake." The music rang out from his PAD, and the huge bee danced.

"You are so cute. Welcome to my home." They were beamed up a ramp into the SpaceHive. Gleaming steel floors and huge rooms were filled with wasps busy at alien computers and other machines. Dark shapes covered the floor near a general bee in uniform.

"What are those?" he asked. "Wow, they're half eaten bees. What was their crime? How did they die?"

His bee captor was silent. Jason faced for the first time the terrible face of General Vard, a huge wasp with a weapon in his hands. He dripped venom and pus came out of his mouth slit.

"Eat him!" The general roared and pitched toward Jason.

"He is beautiful," the young bee repeated. "Please spare my pet."

Jason fainted.

Chapter Eight

I'm still alive, was Jason's first thought when he woke inside the alien room. Honeycombs bordered the walls. He was sockless in his retro Converse tennis shoes. Jason wore his jacket and other clothes. He felt in his pocket for his ZipPAD. His captors hadn't taken it.

"Where am I?" He saw another huge room next to this one and aliens working.

Jason took the PAD out of his pocket. He switched the icon from voice mode to touch and tried to call his father, who would be worried. He'd be searching the area, maybe following his footsteps, unable to help when the trail led to the mother ship.

"I'm on my own now. PAD doesn't work here through the metal walls and electronics. That's why they let me keep it. I'm in the guts of their mother ship. They just dumped me here in a corner of a room." He glanced at his PAD and saw the time. Almost noon. A night and part of a day had gone by.

In the middle of the room there was a cage, a table and a plate of roasted meat with some fruit.

I'm hungry. But will they try to poison me?

Not trying to poison the little pet. He heard the words in his head. Had they read his mind?

Jason tiptoed to the other room. The alien bee queen was eating a plum. A big wasp with a black badge on his chest stood at a control panel.

A smaller bee, though large next to Jason, held a red translator box in her barbed hand. This bee was the same color as the bee he'd met on the path to Cranbrook.

"Please, General Vard, please. Let me keep him."

The wasp turned its black compound eyes toward Jason.

Jason shrank against the door. "Y-you must be the alien leader. My name is Jason Anderson. I'm a student, not a soldier. My father is a famous scientist. They'll be looking for me."

"He is a spy," the wasp hissed into the red box and rattled his barbs.

The other bees, including the queen, didn't pay any attention to Jason.

Jason began to sweat. *I'm trapped and alone. It is very hot in here.*

The friendly bee put her mouth to the red box. "My name is Zibb. I know you are afraid," she buzzed in English.

Jason frowned. *Did she read my mind?*

"I'm your friend," Zibb said. "I think you're beautiful. I'm trying to get the general to let you live."

The wasp turned his back on Jason.

I don't want to be this creature's pet.

He stepped back. The floor was sticky with honey.

"Kill him," Queen Taranta said to the general.

Jason studied the queen. Why was she here with the general in the control room instead of her room? Because the general was amusing? Did a keen mind lie within the queen's huge head? Or a bored one?

"No," Zibb said. "Let's study him. We'll learn about these Earth creatures. He's so different than we are, so we can learn about his race. But he's like us because he's smart and seems to know science. He must know he can't hurt us. Anybody can see that, my queen."

"Worker, stand aside."

"Please. He doesn't have a weapon. He's soft and maybe hungry. He's so cute, General Vard. May I keep him?"

"Well, Worker," the general lashed his poison barbs, "he might amuse us. He's our first captive. We may do surgery on him and then eat him. He doesn't seem fat enough for a good meal though. Why don't you put him in the cell and we'll decide what to do with him then?"

Jason was put in a cage with bars that went eight feet into the air. He was hungry. The meat was still warm on the wooden plate. He saw fruit too.

Zibb patted him on the head as she pulled out a stool from under the table. "Eat, little pet," the translator buzzed. "You have to stay strong."

"Thanks, I guess. I'll have some of this." He sat and began to eat. "Can you tell me where I am?"

He knew he had to find out more about these aliens so he could tell his father when he got out.

"We call this the lab," the huge creature buzzed and patted his head. "Eat, little one."

Jason took another bite. His stomach heaved. He stumbled to the portapoop and threw up.

"Would you like a drink?" Zibb asked.

He groaned, sure they'd given him a roasted rat or something from under a rock. The meat sat like hot lard in his stomach.

"No," he said. "I've had enough."

"Oh, my poor little pet," Zibb said. "Are you all right?"

"Yes," Jason lied.

He stretched out on the cot, trying hard not to throw up again. But his stomach rebelled and emptied his stomach on the floor.

After that, there was only fruit on his table.

"My pet doesn't like meat," Zibb explained the next day to Banter, who had come to Jason's cage to meet the human.

"Odd little thing." Banter danced. "I can't wait to escape this SpaceHive to our great new Jive Hive. Our new home! How long do we have to wait, Zibb?"

"I don't know. It's up to General Vard and how soon the war is won. Lucky it's almost over. Lucky for us, Banter."

"Lucky the general seems to like the odd little human."

"But I know how fast the general can change his mind, and I'm trying to save the pet's life."

"The human won't be safe in this place." Banter glanced at the other room. "The general's too close for comfort."

"Let's be kind to the general. And the queen. They look after the future of our race."

"Yes," Banter agreed, plucking a piece of fuzz from Zibb's orange shoulder. "What of the human?"

"You're right. He won't be safe in this place."

Jason came out of the bathroom where he had been washing up as best he could, and sat at the table. He began to eat pears, plums and green apples. He was very hungry and was a growing boy. Too bad about the meat. He liked roasts. But he couldn't stomach whatever they had tried to feed him. Maybe it was a cat. Or Freedom. He belched.

Zibb and Banter stood together in thought. "Well, General Vard could change his mind. We'll just have to wait and see what happens to my little pet here. He's so cute. I want to keep him."

"We could keep him as a hostage." Banter had the best ideas. "He must have a home somewhere."

"Of course." Zibb scratched her fuzzy chin. "His father might be somebody important."

"Or his mother. He could be a good hostage. He does seem cute."

Zibb slapped Banter between the shoulder blades, where her wings fluttered. "Let's talk it over with the general. My pet's too precious to kill."

"Very cute."

Jason sat in the next room and belched. Maybe it was a roasted cat. A grey cat, like Kitty-Winks. Or something worse. A dog? A rat? What was this strange new world? It wasn't safe to trust his captors. That was plain.

He picked his teeth with the edge of a fingernail.

Chapter Nine

While Jason was trying to figure a way out of the SpaceHive, the earth's leaders were meeting to talk about what to do next. Generals and heads of state from all over the world sat together at a table at the UFN. As his fate was being decided by the wasps in the SpaceHive, so the earth's fate would be decided in these meetings.

A British general spoke first. "We must win the war. No one has come close to the aliens to talk to them so far. Except for the threats from the mother ship when the bees and wasps first landed in British Columbia, we haven't heard any more. They just started killing us and haven't stopped. There must be a way to chat with their leaders, find out what we can do, find out more about them."

President Maria Black spoke next. "Most people on Earth who are still alive are hiding in bunkers and the mother ship and airships do what they want. We're helpless to attack them. We don't know what to do except try a nuclear strike."

The chief of defense, sitting across the table from the president, agreed. "The earth's armed forces can't get through the shields of the wasp ships. Their death rays and war machines have wiped out much of our military, including the armies and navies of North and South America, Europe, Africa, Australia and Asia. You must take yourself and your staff where it's safest, Madam President. The Antarctic is still safe."

President Black shook her head. "Smaller alien airships from the mother ship are killing our planet too. The mother ship controls them. Our people are driven into caves, bunkers and remote mountain areas. Now you say that you want me to take cover in Antarctica? You want me to run and hide?"

A Russian general leaned across the table. "It would be wise to bring a group of scientists and soldiers with you to the Antarctic, President. There's already a scientific base there. It could be used. You'd be safer. We could fight back from here, but our best minds and leaders have to be safe."

"Not many of the aliens have been hurt. Underground bunkers in the hills keep some people safe, but we've lost touch with them. I don't want to leave my people." President Black looked at the Canadian prime minister, whose country had suffered the most damage.

The chief of defense disagreed. "Their war machines send out deadly rays that tear apart the DNA of all living things. Your people want you to be safe, President. It's not weak to go where there is help, Maria. Please listen to us."

"Earth is becoming an Eden," President Black said. "The forests, the tropics are green and lush, strange alien plants are growing in the deserts, the clouds are seeded with a warm rain, winter arrived oddly mild this year."

"Yes, they're changing the weather."

The president continued. "Some wild animals have come back into Eden. Yet men and women live in caves and bunkers, pulling together for the first time, trying to fight back. This may be our last stand. Earth may become a paradise, but without us and at what cost?"

"I spoke my mind already, Maria, many times."

"You're right, Joseph. I never thought offence was the best defence. But there's one more thing to try before I give up and join my family in Antarctica."

"I know what you mean, President. We'll bomb them with nuclear weapons and risk destroying the earth."

"The UFN told me what you plan to do over the hotcom this morning, Joseph. Can we warn our people?"

"What remains of the UFN is doing just that. There'll be a joint strike of the allies. If the mother ship is disabled, the alien airships it controls will be dead ducks in the water too."

"Do it, Joseph. Our planes may take me and the rest of my staff to the Antarctic base. I'll go there if you do as you say and risk destroying our world for a chance to save it. I don't want to destroy any more of Earth, but we have no choice. Bomb them, ladies and gentlemen. That's my vote."

The UFN launched their attack on the mother ship the next day. Jason watched as the screens inside it lit up. He was a prisoner in the ship but allowed to roam freely now. His captors didn't think he was a threat.

"What's happening?" he asked.

"Little pet doesn't want to know." The worker bee Banter held Queen Taranta, who was slurping on honeycomb in the control room.

The Black Watch was busy at the controls of SpaceHive. The huge ship rocked. Its metal walls shook but held firm. The portholes were red with flame. Alien airships rocketed from Central America and Europe to help the SpaceHive and were hit by the nuclear bombs. Yet the airships and SpaceHive did not fall. They were saved by their screens.

Hundreds of nuclear bombs exploded over the Kootenays, carried on Expediter T5 missiles from deep in Colorado at the command of President Black and the chief of defense of the United Federation of Nations. The world's military came together, and Canada was in ruins. Only China remained aloof. The Kootenays, most of Canada and the Northwestern United States were destroyed. Animals and plants were wiped out instantly. The aliens remained inside their ships. They were untouched.

The earth's five-star generals of the UFN were now in charge, and they had failed.

"Told you so," the European prime ministers said. Asia, Africa and the Middle East were silent—their military limped home to nations full of bees and wasps.

"Told you so," Jason said to his bee friend Zibb. "My people will never surrender."

The attack on the mother ship would mean death for the air forces and all humans who remained above ground, but he wasn't afraid to die.

It was all too much for him to think of now.

He looked through the ports, alive with purple lightning, rolling clouds, sheets of grey hail hurled on steaming winds.

"My parents, friends and home buried under radioactive dust, my family's lives in danger."

Jason walked toward the control room.

General Vard looked at him. "You don't feel sorrow and anger at the North American military and their Earth generals who are so short-sighted?"

"I'm only angry at you and your army. You invaded our world."

General Vard's twisted black hole of a mouth appeared to smile. "Your people have just blasted themselves into a fire pit."

"You've lost," Queen Taranta said, sucking on a rotten peach.

General Vard buzzed and hit the controls. The death ray seared the remainder of the UFN airships, and the Expediters exploded in midair.

"Look at that, Earthling."

Deadly radiation rained upon the earth and seeped deep into the soil of North America. Poison clouds and hurricane force winds seared the rest of the world.

"Mayday, mayday!" Jason called into his ZipPAD. "Is anybody there?" But the signal was blocked.

"Give me that, little pet."

"No. It's my only grasp on my life. My family. My friends. You don't understand. You're just an insect."

One of the sergeants took Jason's ZipPAD.

"Give it back!" Jason cried out.

"Only can give it back because the general knows it's harmless, and he has other things on his mind, pet."

"Well, give it back then."

"What are you doing?" Queen Taranta spat at General Vard, who stood at the controls of the death ray and heat guns. "You're destroying our new Jive Hive, the planet that was so green and beautiful until now."

"I'm destroying only what the humans destroyed first." The general's words were like a swamp of poisonous venom.

Jason stared out one of the windows. The ground outside the mother ship was ruined and black, steaming with radiation. The air inside the ship was stuffy, stale, with no chance now of getting clean air from outside.

"We can't stay here in this place much longer," the queen said. "Our filters are groaning with the effort to purify the air."

General Vard scowled. "Obviously the humans have no regard for their environment."

"The only thing we can do, General, is move the ship." Queen Taranta's body shone with sweat. "We're sitting in the middle of a desert worse than the other side of our old Jive Hive we left eight years ago."

"I know, Monarch. The humans did it."

"We tried to make this new Jive Hive a heaven for our kind and wipe out the humans that lived here. We've succeeded only in making it like the other half of Jive Hive at home. The half we don't dare think about now, the deserts on the other side of our planet that forced us to leave."

"You're right, I think," the general rasped. "It would be easy to move the ship. The airships and pods can fly somewhere else too."

"It's not safe here anymore." The queen spat bits of honey-comb on the floor.

"What do you think, pet?" Zibb said. "Where should we go?"

"Try...uh...India. You know how to get to India?"

India was far from the ruins of North America, a garden to delight the senses with oceans in the south and cool mountains in the north. Humanity in India was mostly gone. Only freedom fighters and a few scattered families were left. But India was as far from his family and friends as Jason could imagine. He would try to put distance between the huge ship and those he cared for.

"There's plenty of food there, and India's climate is ideal for life as you know it," he said, hoping to convince General Vard.

"What you call India would be perfect." Queen Taranta rolled her eyes at the general. Honeycomb flew onto the floor from her mouth.

A nurse bent to clean the spot where the queen spat.

"You're brilliant as well as beautiful, my queen," Zibb buzzed.

Jason knew Zibb's comment was meant to please the young monarch. She wanted her queen kept happy and her little human pet safe. He also knew he'd have to go with them when the mother ship lifted to the other side of the earth.

"It will be done." General Vard gave orders and stood at the console, a dark figure outlined in dim blue lights.

"What's going on?" Jason asked.

"The mother ship's moving to the other side of the world, to the place you call India."

"Am I safe?" he asked of his only friend on the ship. "Maybe the general's in a good mood, a good sign for me. I don't want to go to the other side of the earth. But I will if it means protecting my family and friends if they're not dead already."

"Many dead, little pet."

"I need to stay alive, Zibb. I might be the only human left in North America. I need to avenge my race."

"I'll keep you safe, little pet," Zibb assured him.

Banter stood nearby and rolled her compound eyes. "Yes, you'll come with us to this place called India."

"I've always wanted to see South Asia," Jason said. "If the radiation doesn't expand from the Kootenays to the rest of the globe. Do you know the way to India?"

Banter let out a small huff. "Our computer navigates for us."

"Yes. I think that India is a good idea," Zibb said. "We've run it through our telescans. Looks great. Let's go."

Jason turned on his ZipPAD. "Mayday," he shouted into the channel he and his parents had chosen. "Mayday!"

The bees were amused.

"Mom? Dad? Come in."

"He thinks they're still alive."

The Black Watch taunted him, but the aliens continued to allow him to move freely about the ship as they prepared to leave the Purcell Mountains in British Columbia.

General Vard gave orders. Miles below, the Purcell Mountains tipped and left the alien general's screen. The ship locked onto the magnetic poles of the earth and rose. Its shadow covered all of western Canada and the northwestern USA. Superconductors whined and screeched. They locked on latitude and longitude. The ship rocketed far into space, whirled and shattered the sound barrier landing minutes later in a distant mountain area of India called Himachal Pradesh.

The population of Himachal Pradesh had fled to the caves with the first wave of alien ships. No one lived on the plains or towns.

"Our Black Watch is pleased with India," Zibb said. "We worker bees, nurses and drones were told we could leave the ship right away to explore and eat fresh food, collect nectar for honey, stretch our legs in a forest that's like our old Jive Hive."

"The area is ideal." Queen Taranta preened. "We chose well. There are snowy mountains in the north to hide the ship, rivers and trees, tropics in the south and types of animals which have not yet been driven away as the area is so remote. There's plenty of fresh water now."

The great ship sucked up water, running cold and sweet from the Himalaya Mountains. Robot scrubs were set around the outside of the ship to mop up radiation. The wasps opened the doors and ports to let in fresh air.

"We can hang meat and have ripe fruit," the queen said, her antennae twitching at the thought of good food. "We can make more honey and royal jelly."

Zibb and her cousins jumped up and down, flapping their arms. "We'll feed the queen sweet nectar and find her a nice palace with honey stored in wax honeycombs."

"I'm pleased," General Vard remarked. "You've done well to choose this India place, human."

"Pardon, General?" Saliva oozed from the corner of the queen's mouth.

"Excuse me. Of course it was my queen whose great advice I followed."

Later in the day, the bees had a chance to roam through the countryside and gather fruit and meat. When they beamed back to the ship, Zibb went to Jason's cage. Zibb put a wooden bowl of breadfruit, custard apples, mangoes and Burmese grapes on his table.

"Thank you," he said.

The red box clicked. "You're welcome, little pet. I hope you enjoy the treats." Zibb stroked Jason's mop of hair with a barbed hand. The great bee stood for a moment longer, as though trying to make up her mind about something. Her stubby wings fanned the air behind her.

"What is it?" he asked. "Is there news?" Sometimes Zibb would tell him stories of the outside world. Jason listened for clues of how the war went. Humanity may have lost the war within the first few weeks of conquest by the alien general and his troops. He knew well enough the destruction of North America. He had seen it through the screens, had felt the great vessel rock, had heard Zibb's comments. The nuclear strike by the American and UFN military caused the mother ship to move and nothing more, but the attack ruined the area around Cranbrook and Creston, and most of the continent.

Zibb was silent for a moment, then said, "I'm worried about General Vard." She stood by Jason's cage. The translator whirred.

"Why? Does he want to kill me? And pick my bones?"

"Well," Zibb said. "Now that you mention it..."

"Don't worry." Jason picked at a piece of breadfruit. "I'm glad we've moved to India. It means my parents and friends, if any remain, will be safer now that you're gone from the mountains around our home. They'll be working on a way to defeat you," he warned. *And so am I.* His captors didn't pick up the thought although sometimes it seemed to the boy they could read his mind.

"If they're alive." A nearby lieutenant mocked him. "What we have not done with our war machine, the generals of North America have with their nuclear missiles and silly guerrilla warfare."

"I'll save the earth." Jason thought of the thousands of miles that separated him from home. He thought of how the music had calmed Zibb that first night and drugged the huge bee into a dance in the forest by Yahk in the moonlight.

Jason glanced at his PAD. It would play music with the touch of a button. They allowed him to play games on it during the day as he wandered about the huge rooms. He couldn't receive on it. There was only a message that said "out of range."

Jason frowned. No one appeared to have thought about what he might do or think. Too busy with their labs, screens and crowding about the open door of the ship when they could. Too busy avoiding the notice of their vicious wasp general and his Black Watch—too busy avoiding their greedy queen.

Very well. They didn't seem to consider him any sort of threat at all.

"Why would you consider me a threat?"

He was a boy, alone, unarmed, surrounded by millions of aliens where Earth's entire military might had failed, captive in a mother ship that threatened everyone.

"What, pet?"

"Uh…I'm just thinking out loud."

"How do you think out loud, little soft morsel of flesh?"

"Like a translator."

"Oh…"

Jason had a plan. He would have to be cool headed, fast thinking and use his emotions. Look out for *numero uno*. But he was doing this for a greater purpose. Earth was number one right now.

Cogito ergo sum. My father was smart. Is smart. Like father, like son. Wish I'd listened more. Is smart. Present tense. Dad's not dead. Give me strength.

Zibb looked at him fondly, brought him fresh fruit, honey and other treats for meals, and seemed to Jason to be the perfect model for the next test.

"Zibb?"

"Yes, little pet?"

"You like music?"

"Oh! The Music of the Wings, the dance, oh yes. Yes. Back home. You know more of that music, little pet? Like the first night in the forest? On your amusing little instrument there?"

"Yes."

The chance came sooner than Jason thought. He needed an alien he could trust not to kill him if his plan went wrong.

There was only one clear choice.

Chapter Ten

"I uber-loaded a googlegig of music last summer," Jason said to his only friend on the skyship. "Music which might make my listeners hurt somebody if we're not careful."

"Hurt somebody, pet? Not me. Not Zibb."

"There was only you, Zibb, dancing that first night to the rock music. If I stood in the middle of Queen Taranta and her wasp soldiers, hurled an awesome bass into the room, or a hip-hop rock song, or even a new jazz, what would happen? Would they lay their weapons down, open the doors for us, allow us to dance out on the plains of Himachal Pradesh and run to the caves?"

"That's your plan, pet? I don't know. I must think about that."

To find perhaps the local freedom fighters? Zibb seemed to agree. Freedom! To find scientists and a lab, to discover a sound that would control even the general and his troops. Maybe to win the war? It was not likely to happen, but it was worth putting the PAD to the test. A long shot.

Music. *Music of the Wings* echoed Zibb in his mind. It could be done.

He thought of a quote his mother had taught him, "Only those who risk going too far can possibly find out how far they can go."

The huge ships, the energy drives, the shockwaves, the earthquakes and tsunamis—the world was in chaos. The coast and North Vancouver were gone. Victoria gone, Kamloops gone,

Prince George in the northeast maybe had been spared, but all of Alberta had been obliterated by the war machine. The rest of Canada was battered, hiding. The United States too.

Alien ships inhabited Mexico and South America, Europe, Asia, Australia and Africa. The mother ship was pulsing her energy, hatred and death. Most of humanity was dead, the rest scattered, hiding, fighting back with hand weapons and flying air scooters. So many dead. *Millions* dead.

"My parents might be dead," he told Zibb.

"You mourn for your parents, pet? You think they're dead?"

"Almost for sure. I wish I could mourn them better. But mostly I wish I could have them back, the world back, the way it was. I won't think of it."

His mother, his unborn brother, Kitty-Winks and the robotess might be safe in the underground bunkers which were surrounded by radioactive clouds. They would be unable to come out though.

His mother could someday shake her son's hand. "Thanks for taking care of yourself," she'd say. "Thanks for saving the world, Jay."

And they'd all go home.

He didn't want to think of the lab in Yahk and what almost for sure happened to his father. No, they'd go home, the *four* of them—his father, mother, baby brother and him. Just like things used to be, but with a healthy baby brother too.

"Don't think of it, little pet. Wasp General busy now, blasting orders into space, other airships follow, blast your world. Maybe not good for us, either. We worker bees want to settle here in peace."

General Vard heard them from the next room. He was leaning on the controls next to his majors and the second lieutenant. The wasp sergeants surrounded the queen and her nurses, the ship rocked with the force of explosions and shouted orders blasting into space, many times louder over huge speakers.

"We come in peace." General Vard grinned and spit dribbled from the side of his slimy jaw. "You'll be in pieces soon, Earthling, if not already. Your world shot to the death, blasted core of it melted."

A wrong decision now would ruin everything. A broken melody, a guitar out of tune, a sour tone and all would be lost. Jason couldn't predict the wasps' behavior. But he had discovered their secret, which no one else in the world knew.

Music.

"What, pet? Music? Oh, yes."

Music would calm the aliens like a lullaby to babies. If the aliens killed him, the earth would be lost. But General Vard's nasty soldiers were busy, not paying attention to Jason and his plans.

Ignorant wasps. He smiled. *No, not ignorant. Smart wasps, but not giving humanity enough credit for brains and guts.*

A big mistake when it came to mankind.

Jason opened a small panel in the ZipPAD and took out some earbuds. They were plugged into the PAD. He adjusted them in his ears and chose the more innocent of his music.

He needed to select the perfect song, one that wouldn't incite rage.

Hip-hop? Rock? Those were definitely out.

Music is mathematical and math is built on logic. Music is built on numbers. I want to affect the cells in their brains. I have to use logic. What should I play?

He sorted through the choices and thought hard. What would tame and finally destroy the wasps and their followers?

He needed something soothing and hypnotic.

I have it! Brahms!

His mother loved it and had insisted on downloading for him that day last spring when they had all been together in their cozy house in Creston, before he and his father moved to Yahk, before Jason disappeared into the forest.

Brahms would work. He just knew it.

He wasn't sure his ZipPAD was set the way it should be for his plan. The ZipPAD was new and he'd been too busy to read all the instructions

The menu scrolled down the screen through a long list of songs.

Scrolling…

Then…

Brahms's Third Symphony. Yes!

He selected the song. The music made him smile. It swelled, ebbed and flowed, and even he felt calmer. It was a happy song.

I must calm the bees.

But first, he had to test his theory that music would affect them.

There was one bee that maybe he could trust. One bee that might not kill him if he were wrong. And if he made the wrong choice, they'd destroy the rest of the earth as he knew it. If he selected the wrong music, it might stir up the wasps to destroy him too.

Jason found Zibb in the control room talking to Banter and trying to stay out of the way. General Vard strode from one console to the next. The Black Watch was a blur of action, sabres and barbs rattling. They left the landscape in India around Space-Hive intact. But they were very angry.

The robots had finished mopping up the radiation on the ship. He didn't have much time.

"Zibb. Listen to this."

Chapter Eleven

"Zibb, come with me." Jason danced in front of the friendly alien, heels thudding, *dunna dunna dunna*. Zibb was curious, not yet hearing the music which swelled into Jason's earbuds. Banter stayed where she was.

"Stay here," Zibb told Banter.

She followed Jason. "What does little pet want with the little box that makes music? So nice, the music. What next?"

She hopped behind Jason into his cage, where he put the earbuds on her hearing slits and turned up the PAD. She gazed at him and her black eyes softened. Her antennae twitched. He wondered if he should wink at her.

He was unprepared for the reaction, but should have expected it.

She let out a high-pitched buzz, so excited and happy. "This is like the songs we had back on our old Jive Hive. This is magic."

Jason teased her with Poco Allegretto, from Symphony in F Major, Op. 90. "Brahms, Zibb. You have never heard Brahms? You don't know what you've missed."

The keening strings, the bold horns, the clarinets. The notes of the flute soared like birds over the top of the staff. Zibb tore off the earbuds and began to buzz with excitement. She hugged her small human friend. "My little king. Are you hungry? You are so thin."

She skipped to the royal rooms next door. She came out with a wooden bowl of royal jelly. "Eat this, my dear little pet."

The jelly in the wooden bowl looked like coconut cream.

Jason placed the earbuds back in their case and smiled. He was losing weight on his new diet of only fruit. His clothes hung loose on his frame. He'd heard of royal jelly and its benefits.

"This is good," Jason said as Zibb spooned the royal jelly into his mouth. It *did* taste like coconut.

Zibb smiled and spooned more royal jelly into his mouth.

"What are you doing, Zibb? What's the noise? Why, you're dancing." Banter swayed in the doorway.

Jason turned up the volume and set the external speakers to play. He swallowed more royal jelly.

Banter and Zibb joined four of their arms and began to dance together. A wasp sergeant-at-arms danced into the room, followed by another. *Wasps. Same thing.* They bowed, scraped their hairy legs together, jumped up and down, hugged him and spooned royal jelly into his mouth. It was sweet like honey. He ate hungrily.

"We're starving our new friend. Eat."

They were joined by others. The music of Brahms swelled and hung in the room. Jason could smell roasting meat. Another soldier joined them, carrying a platter with wooden utensils.

"Roast bird," Zibb's red translator crackled.

Zibb spooned more royal jelly into his mouth and cut a breadfruit into pieces with a laser beam. They set the roast pheasant in front of Jason. They skipped and danced. He ate, his belt becoming tighter around his middle. The meat was good.

"You need more clothing, little pet," Zibb said. "You're so thin your clothes don't fit anymore. Eat. I'll see what I can do."

"Maybe let me out on the plains into the Indian towns. I'd like to find a *kurta* that would fit me and some loose white pants. They'd be cooler than these jeans and dirty shirt."

"I'll see what I can do." Zibb danced. "You want human company, little pet? *Buzz, buzz, buzz.* Maybe we find nice girl pet for you?"

"No. But thanks. I'll find my own girl in time." Jason moved his index finger, selecting flamenco guitars from the music on his ZipPAD. The music was fast and bright.

Zibb took Banter's upper arm and did a bee imitation of a Spanish fandango, snapping her barbs.

The sounds from the PAD changed, but continued to enchant the bees and wasps. The flutes swelled. The strings moaned. The clarinets crooned. There was a ZitherCom also, a new instrument for uber-modern orchestras.

The bee creatures whirled. Banter stomped and laughed out loud into Zibb's translator. They broke apart, breathless—loving Jason, loving one another.

"I want the war over and I want things back the way they were," Jason said. *It's working.* The bees had lost control. The bass pounded in his ears.

General Vard appeared in the doorway. He was not amused.

"Guards. Sergeants-at-arms." he roared. "Spike them! Eat them! Way-out rabble." Zibb's translator picked up the anger in the general's voice. The dancing stopped. More soldiers poured into the room.

Jason chose a tune by the Four Dirty Skulls and turned up the volume. The wasp soldiers began to sway. General Vard thundered, flinging poison barbs into the necks of the nearest soldiers.

"Get them! Stop that racket." The general waved his hands into the air. "Or I'll kill you myself."

The music swelled. The ZipPAD began to crackle. Something strange and wonderful was happening in that room. La la la...oh, oh, oh. Then more clarinets, an oboe, electronic guitar and louder ZitherCom. The entire room began to shake.

Jason's fingers moved over the PAD. The On power light glowed. The shields must be down on the ship because the PAD was receiving. The ZipPAD crackled.

More static. The Send/Receive button glowed green, even in the bright lights of the room.

"Namaste." The voice was male and heavily accented.

The creatures in the room were still bipping and bopping, they hummed and buzzed. General Vard was furious.

Jason spoke into the PAD. "Do you speak English? I don't believe it."

"Yes," the human voice replied. "I am very excited to meet you, too."

"Give me that," General Vard roared.

Jason dodged the wasp's angry lunge and moved around the room, keeping the others between him and the general. The noise was deafening. Wasps and workers linked arms and danced together. His music was no longer necessary as the wasps had lost control.

Zibb kissed him on the top of his head. She danced away, arms linked with a soldier.

Jason spoke into the glowing PAD to the Indian voice, scarcely daring to breathe. He couldn't believe his luck. He ran to the privacy of his cage, dodging the general and his troops. He sat on the edge of his cot, hands cupped over the ZipPAD, which he held to his ear. "I know a bit of Hindustani. But can we speak English? There may not be much time, friend. I need your help."

"I'm freedom fighter. You have soldiers to help us?"

Jason struggled to hear. There seemed to be a fight going on with the Black Watch still loyal to the general. The queen was out of sight, her nurse bees in the far room. He saw the prancing figures of the worker bees and soldiers near his cage.

"You American?" the voice asked.

"No, but close. Canadian. Who are you?"

"My name is Aadab Ali. May Allah be praised. I'm young Indian, take engineering courses, want to go to engineering college, but aliens come."

Jason sighed. "I'm sorry. But we don't have a lot of time, Aadab. You can be sure I'm your friend. I'm very glad to meet you." The noise in the two rooms of the skyship continued and it was hard to talk or listen.

"You from the fifty-fourth state?"

"No." Jason explained about Canada. "North of Washington state, north of Michigan, north of Montana."

"Nothing's north of Montana," the voice said. "Only polar bears."

"No polar bears in Creston." Jason took a deep breath. "I need your help. The world needs your help. No matter where you're from. Or me."

Jason knew it was no longer important what country anyone came from since all countries of Earth were now united against a common enemy, at war with aliens that could wipe humans from the planet.

There were no borders.

"I am freedom fighter for the world," Aadab said. "Phir Bhi Pil Hai Hindustani."

Static crackled and flared.

"Bad connection, man." Aadab's voice faded in and out. "Where...you? How...I...help?"

"I'm in an alien ship," Jason said, lowering his voice and watching the bees and wasps. "We're in your country."

""You...India?"

"Yes. Listen, I can track you and call you back if we get disconnected. I can find you again."

The green power light went out. The line was dead.

General Vard pushed past a wasp lieutenant, who was trying to keep back the crowd. The bee workers continued to dance, though the music had stopped.

"Fools," the general roared.

Jason staggered to the barred walls of his cage and closed the door. He punched buttons on the Zip. *Drums? Clarinets? Guitars? BlastStrings, an even newer instrument than the ZitherCom?*

He needed something inspiring.

Ah-ha! Got it!

The Canadian national anthem swelled into the room. He recalled watching an Olympic women's hockey game eighteen months ago. Those were happier times. A time when the world was united, but not against an enemy. He'd been proud of Canada's achievements back then.

The true North, strong and free...from far and wide, Oh Canada...

The crowd of bees and wasps went wild.

Jason sang along. "Oh Canada, glorious and *free...*"

Queen Taranta waddled into the room. Leaning on a nurse, her body swollen, she chewed on a piece of honeycomb that was dripping with royal jelly.

"What are you doing?" she buzzed into her translator. "You wish to play?"

General Vard snorted. "Behold your fools, your majesty."

"Music of the Wings," one of the worker bees sang. "At last."

They danced as though they had never left the old Jive Hive.

Jason had never seen them look so happy.

Chapter Twelve

"Hello? Anybody there, man? This is freedom fighter in Uttar Pradesh, India, calling. My name, Aadab Ali, Allah be praised. Anybody want to come help?" There was no response from his homeland, only from other countries with like tales of ruin and death.

Aadab monitored the airwaves, picking up static and broadcasts from all over the world, all of them the same. The invaders had destroyed the land, and the people were helpless against them.

He had kept the power going in the small village of Hardiwar on his return, even after most of the village was burned. He thought there might be other Indians who would be attracted to the lights.

Then he thought of the bees.

"They also would be attracted by the lights if they come back," he muttered. "I think it smarter that I stay here in the caves of the hill country and go out only at dusk. I noticed the aliens to be mostly quiet and sleepy then. Maybe the rainy weather keeps them in their ships too."

Many airships had left recently. He thought many of the smaller alien ships had been called back to the SpaceHive. "Something bad must be going on."

Roar!

The sound was like thunder.

Rrrroarr!

A massive ship blackened the noon sky. The mother ship was here.

Aadab stood and watched the SpaceHive as it crossed the border northwest in the direction of Himachal Pradesh.

"I'm freedom fighter now, fierce yet gentle and a good man. My girlfriend Iodine loves such a man. I'm twenty years old and she is sixteen, perfect ages. How happy I am to find a girl like Iodine. Allah be praised, but I must send her away now, to the farther hills where she will be safe like my parents and sisters."

He kept a copy of the Koran in his hip pocket at all times and prayed five times a day with his face to the east. He prayed then, watching the great ship cross his country and fall to earth out of his sight. He went to find Iodine in the cave with the old couple who looked after her.

"There should be a mosque to pray with my brothers," he explained to old Wajeeha, who was too old to fight or pray or care, and to Wajeeha's wife, Gailine, who cared for the lovely Iodine.

Aadab explained his feelings to the girl as they walked together down the paths from the caves where Wajeeha and Gailine sat inside over a low fire and had glared at the young lovers as Iodine and Aadab had left together.

"Your face is not hidden by a *hijab*, your metallic jeans and cotton shirts are uber-modern. You are shy girl yet bold at the same time. I don't know what to make of you, Iodine, but I love you. I'm glad you were spared out of all the village young women."

There was silence, only the crush of stones under their feet as they walked the trail.

"Iodine?"

"Yes"

"We're a perfect match, if only your father would agree."

"I have no father now, but old Wajeeha and Gailine, and they don't like the match."

"Times are different."

"Wajeeha and his wife are old school. They don't like my open face and slim jeans, the tight tops."

"She of the hard eyes like a hip-hop rock star."

Iodine laughed. "They don't like you, Aadab Ali. For one thing, you are not the same religion."

"I'm very, very sad that my beloved is a different faith."

Could they possibly be a couple? He was Northern Indian and Muslim, she was Southern and Hindi. He often thought of Iodine when he was away from the caves. Sometimes she'd mock him. Devil little girl with angel eyes.

Aadab squatted in the elephant grass near the small stream one day, preparing to return to his cave, when he heard his SmartPAD ring.

"Hello?" A human voice. The PAD stuttered again. Aadab had set the homing signal to pick up any contact from a PAD within five hundred miles from him and then lock onto it. Aadab heard music and a young voice.

"Namaste," Aadab said. *Greetings.* The voice he heard sounded American, for sure not Urdu or Indian or European. "There may not be much time, friend. I need your help."

Aadab thumbed the controls of his old SmartPAD. The signal on the scope became stronger. The location was northwest of here, in the next state of Himachal Pradesh or maybe even Nepal.

He could track the location of the American using the GPS device in his SmartPAD, of course, as the American could also track him. However, there seemed to be a lot of static. "Is there a party going on?"

The signal was weak. Aadab would guess the American was safe in a concrete or steel house, perhaps even under the ground. Aadab was excited. At last, there was help.

"Glad to meet you, American boy." Aadab ran his fingers through his gleaming mat of black hair.

"I'm Canadian," the young voice said. "It was my country the UFN bombed."

Canadian? Was there anything north of Montana but polar bears and igloos? Later Aadab learned a geography lesson from Jason Anderson.

The connection was broken but not before Aadab noted the number and locked onto the location of his new friend.

He started back toward the caves in the hills. Excitement grew.

"I've found some help!"

Humming, Aadab climbed the steep path to his home. For the first time he didn't glance over at the slopes a quarter of a mile away where Iodine often walked after dinner. His eyes swept the sky instead. The rainy season was not over. The sun was covered with clouds and gusts of wind would bring more rain.

Shivering, Aadab pulled aside the bamboo curtain and strode to the dead ashes of his campfire in the back of his cave. "My *kurta's* wet."

He wrung out his shirt and stoked the fire with dry wood. His Quik Flint flared, and the wood began to burn. He thumbed the SmartPAD again but this time there was no answer.

"I hope the Canadian has an army behind him. Even so, we alone could save the world. Me and the stranger." The stranger sounded young and smart, like Aadab. "We'll save India and the world. My heart belongs to my country first though."

Aadab Ali ate a simple meal of breadfruit and fish, and then called the number he had locked on. A voice answered.

"Hello, Jason. You ready to tell me the truth about your country now? You're not the fifty-fourth state?" Aadab laughed. "I have small air scooter, man. I take it to the mother ship in Himachal Pradesh tomorrow. Me and my weapons."

"Plan to arrive at dusk, when the aliens are most sleepy. Later we'll hatch our plans, you and I."

"Me and your polar bears, Jason."

Aadab had prayed to Allah for help, and now it was here. But how would they do it? Two young men and their PADs, a laser rifle and an Everbeam. "I thought you had an army. I thought you were rescuing me. Now I have to rescue you. But my heart belongs to the world. My heart belongs to polar bears too. We'll do it."

Meanwhile, in his cot in the SpaceHive, Jason laughed and said, "Yes, my Indian friend, we'll do it." He prepared for sleep.

Zibb and Banter held weapons and stood guard over General Vard in the next room. The general had been taken captive the night before.

"The Black Watch is toast," Jason said with a smug grin.

The worker bees, soldiers and bee drones, driven by their anger with their leaders, had taken the General's loyal wasps as prisoners.

"We won the war on Earth," the workers and drones buzzed, "and now we'll have a party. Fields of clover and nectar are out there. No longer will we be under the control of the wasps, those mean leaders who eat rotting meat and start wars."

The queen screamed, "Cowards! Traitors!"

She buzzed in her cage near General Vard's jail, while a drone fed her royal jelly through the bars.

Jason had eaten a meal of breadfruit, leftover pheasant and royal jelly that evening. He was feeling well. *I'm busy as a bee.* He smiled as he lay down on the cot in his cage. *I know there's a lot to do yet to win our freedom.*

The real war had just begun.

Chapter Thirteen

In the SpaceHive Jason moaned and turned on his back. He dreamed he was wearing a cotton shirt, or *kurta*, and loose white pants. He dreamed he danced with the great god, Shiva, of India. His father had taught him of other faiths, so he knew about the Hindu Supreme Being. Shiva was a Hindu god who created the world.

Allahu akbar. Khatim al-nabiyyin. His father had taught him some Urdu, which Aadab spoke. *There is none but Allah.* Why were the Muslim words in a dream about a Hindu god?

In his sleep, he heard Aadab's prayers. Not only did he hear them, he saw the man in his dream, in a cave near the plains of Himachal Pradesh, half-asleep beneath a red blanket. And he understood the foreign words.

The high notes of a flute hung and wailed above his head. In his dream, he whirled and stamped out ignorance in the form of a cobra snake. The world was created again like a lotus flower in Shiva's navel. Shiva held a golden sword.

My heart belongs to the world.

The Muslim words began to fade, but the lotus and god glowed in his mind. The cobra swallowed the lotus and turned on the god. Jason lay helpless in his dream, trying to scream to wake up.

The cobra opened its mouth, and its fangs dripped with poison. The snake looked at him and slithered toward him. The god placed the golden sword in Jason's hand and he cut open the black hooded head of the snake. Its thick yellow blood soaked his body.

I've killed it!

He had never felt so powerful.

Around midnight, he woke with a shudder in his cage in the alien ship. Then he slept again, without dreams, until morning when Zibb appeared at his door with more pheasant and fruit.

"Let's open the doors of this ship and get outside and play."

"Sure," Zibb said. "We tied up the wasps. Queen Taranta is helpless in her cage. We feed her well. Long live the queen. Our friends are taking apart the screens and war machine. It's not all up to us two, little pet. We have friends. We've earned our freedom on the plains. Let's go, *waa-hooo.*"

Thousands of bee workers and drones beamed down to the fields of Himachal Pradesh from the great mother ship. The bees danced and gathered fruit and nectar, rolled in fields of bright flowers, splashed in rivers. Jason and Zibb danced together with them.

He kept his PAD open to the channel shared with Aadab. He told his new friend about the dream and the snake who had tried to swallow a god.

"What does your dream mean, Canadian boy? Maybe the snake means the aliens from a very bad place, and the lotus or god is the earth."

"I think the dream was asking me if I was willing to destroy the aliens."

"Are you?" Aadab asked.

"You know the answer," Jason said. "You feel the same way. We'll do what's needed to save our families and friends."

"And the world."

Jason swallowed hard. "Yes. And the world."

"Have the leaders of Earth's nations failed, with only two young men of different countries to win a great war using music and PADs and science?"

Jason stared at the alien bees around him as they danced and made their own music with rough reeds found on the plain. "It looks like it's just us, Aadab. At least for now."

General Vard rattled his barbs and strode about the cage, guarded by workers who stayed far away from him. He was so angry he wanted to spike each and every last one of them. Including that blasted human.

"You'll need me again!" he bellowed. "Just wait and see, you worthless dripping fodder of bog slimes. I'll be there to help you out of this one, and you'll beg me to help you. I'll stick you all with black venom and eat your guts while you're alive."

But first, you'll beg for your lives.

Chapter Fourteen

The United Federation of Nations on Earth was aware of the location of the mother ship and not as helpless as the wasps thought. Most of North America was a howling nuclear desert. Its remaining above-ground citizens, including President Black, the Canadian prime minister and Professor Stephen Anderson, had been sent to the Antarctic on rocket planes and mega-copters. Many of the scientific and military groups that survived joined them later in the Antarctic.

Europe was presently the strongest continent, followed by Asia and Australia. The leadership now fell to the Dutch.

General Joseph Zellers of the UFN continued to advise attack.

"Instruct my counterpart in Holland, or what remains of Holland, to attack the ship where it hides in Himachal Pradesh." His junior aide rushed to the red hotputer to obey.

The Dutch got together with their allies that were left across Europe, Australia and Africa.

As Jason and his bee friends danced on the plains of India, great European war planes took off into clear skies.

"Pretty flowers, little pet," Zibb said.

His light *kurta* ballooned with the evening breeze. Zibb, Banter and Bipp surrounded him dancing, rasping like deep bass fiddles as they threw flowers into the air.

The Dutch bombed them first, being the leaders. The worker bees watched the bombs blossom on the plains of India.

"Our great ship SpaceHive is down without screens, the death rays are quiet, our war machine not working until somebody turns it on again. Our general and soldiers are in chains."

"We're soft round targets, happy on the plains of Himachal Pradesh, hands full of fruit and not death rays."

Tasty globes of fruit in their barbed hands, feet dancing through the tall grass into the jungles farther south, none of the bees could fly in the earth's heavy gravity. They fled in their minipods to caves and mountains in Himachal Pradesh, but the bombs followed them.

The sound of alien minipods landing in the hills around him awakened Aadab. On this starless night, Aadab's old SmartPAD glowed by his side. He flicked on his BrightBeam and locked onto the Dutch channel.

"Come here with all the bombs you got. Your laser guns too, or what remains of them. The aliens are roosted birds, sir, helpless on the ground. My name is Aadab Ali. I'm freedom fighter for the world. I'm from India, here in Himachal Pradesh, just come find us. Lock on my voice, man."

"We're on our way, boy," the Dutch assistant said. "Bombs have now landed."

"Crazy Canadian boy with music is on plains outside ship, and lots of aliens on our side. Come quick. We'll win the war. But don't bomb us, man. Bomb the ship. Very bad aliens in ship."

"Ja," the Dutch General said. He used the translator on his PAD. "They'll come—the allies I can put together quickly, Aadab. Europe and Asia. We're there already. Ja. You must hear the planes."

"Holland rocks." Aadab ran to his air scooter to join the fight.

They roared overhead within a few minutes, the Expeditor T-5s, the old Hawkeyes with their solar-guided warheads, the young fresh pilots and the jaded colonels, all that was left of the world's forces were coming to the aid of their planet Earth to this northern state of India.

Jason was on the plain near the SpaceHive, when the second wave of bombs fell.

"What the heck?" He clenched his fists and kept the channel with Aadab open.

"You get away from that mother ship," Aadab said. "I've locked on your location with SmartPAD. Get away from the plains. Can you hide in hole in ground, in cave, in forest?"

"I can't." The green Send/Receive button glowed on Jason's ZipPAD. "The bombs are all around us. The bees who didn't escape in pods at the first outbreak of the battle are running in all directions, some back to the ship, others to the forest for cover. They're slow in Earth's denser gravity."

The crash of bombs and the sizzle of the laser guns as flames struck soft flesh were so loud that Aadab could probably hear it through the airwaves. Would the Dutch and allied planes be a match against the millions of aliens in SpaceHive and the airships?

Soon more human freedom fighters poured in from across the border in the Sikh territory, from Nepal and from the city of New Delhi. Later, men and women came in armoured trucks from as far south as Sri Lanka. They crossed the Gulf of Mannar on big ships.

Homemade flamethrowers in allied hands flared and flashed. Great pieces of shrapnel ballooned from shoulder guns, and handheld weapons sputtered death into the middle of the aliens.

"They're going back to their soldiers for help, Aadab Ali." Jason saw his bee friends swarm to the huge SpaceHive and howl to be beamed up. Their airships dotted the sky.

The Greeks and French arrived. The Russians said they were on their way. They said the Tibetans were planning their own attack. The nations had no time for planning this together at high levels. The Finns dropped from the sky on sport paragliders. A group from Zimbabwe and the Sudan got together with the Austrians in armoured trucks lowered from big megacopters.

"Sikh, Indian and Pakistani soldiers are coming to help us from their hiding places in the mountains and farther south." Jason's PAD intercepted human military voices, in the world's common languages of English, Bengali, Urdu and Hindustani, with demands to give up.

"We give up. Don't hurt us," the alien drones, workers and nurses called from the caves in the hills, mountains, forests and plains of Northern India.

"No, man, don't hurt the bees on the plains," Aadab said. "They are good aliens. Bomb the ship, man. Bomb the wasps, airships and pods. Take them down, man. Leave the plains alone. There are good aliens on the plains and now in caves in the mountains. Don't hunt them down, Dutchman. This can be end of war if we all work together. Listen to my voice."

Bombs continued to fall. Human ground forces surged into the open.

The shining metal doors of the great mother ship gaped open. A huge roar shook Himachal Pradesh—more than the noise of bombs, human war machines and laser rockets. The bees that were still on the plains and in forests beamed back into their SpaceHive. Their minipods returned from the hills to dock with the great mother ship.

The bees were frightened, rattled and helpless. General Vard stood outlined against the flames. The great war machine was beside him. The soldiers who had released him were in the doorway behind the evil shape of their general.

"Kill them all!" the general commanded.

The war machine poked its snout from an opening in the SpaceHive.

"Aim and fire, you low-life, scum-sucking bladder tumors!"

The Black Watch, who had released General Vard from jail, aimed the war machine and heat guns at the allied planes and the human foot soldiers.

"Aim high! Blow them from the sky."

The Black Watch moved the muzzles of the death rays up to where the allied planes flew. Flaming hunks of metal fell to the earth. Fireworks lit up the sky. Heat guns sliced through the foot soldiers of Earth like knives through soft cheese.

The Dutch planes and their allies in the sky turned and fled. The Sudanese forced their way into the SpaceHive along with the screaming aliens who came back from the plains to be safe in the ship.

Queen Taranta looked over General Vard's shoulder. Her white sluggish body rippled with alarm. "Get in here, you rotten excuses for life. Run, fly, jump! There's safety here, although you don't deserve it."

The wasp general went back to the controls of the SpaceHive and sealed the screens when the last of the bees had re-entered the ship. "Lift into the air and blast the human armies with all the power you wormy underlings can muster."

The ship roared into the flaming sky, but the Sudanese army was already inside the ship, a handful of worker aliens by their side. The earth bees escaped from their hives on the mother ship and stung mindlessly. Two human soldiers, who were allergic to the venom, dropped to the metal planks of the ship.

"Banter!" Zibb called from inside the control room of Space-Hive.

"Here."

Zibb looked around for Banter and found her moving Queen Taranta to a safer place with a guard of nurse bees.

Jason had been left behind on the plain. Zibb's mind raced for Jason's mind, locked on his thought patterns and glowed with warmth, comfort and peace.

My little pet, are you safe?

Surprised, he replied in his mind from the forest outside. *Yes, my friend.*

Play the music, Zibb communicated. *Play it now. Loud. My translator is locked to your PAD and the volume is as high as it will go.*

Jason's hands moved over the ZipPAD and turned the volume to high. He played the latest song from Angela Lu and her band. The sound was deafening and the bees danced throughout the SpaceHive.

"Stop!" General Vard roared as he stood at the controls of the ship.

The Four Dirty Skull's Ninth Symphony was next.

Jason cranked the volume louder.

"Stoppppp!"

It was too much for the wasp general to take. He tensed at the ship's controls, enraged by the dancing going on around him, at the bees turning against him, at the Sudanese on their knees being fed royal jelly.

"I'll teach you all to mutiny, and I'll show you, Earthling scum." General Vard aimed the death ray inside his ship at his queen's own subjects. "Traitors," he cried.

The death ray blazed into the ship, swept across the control room and, for the three or four minutes it was turned on, melted all weapons and walls inside SpaceHive.

The mother ship hovered in the air, began to shoot skyward, then stopped in midair and broke apart. Flames blazed from all ports.

"Help us, Aadab and Jason!" the worker bees screamed over the translators.

Jason cringed. "I can't help my friends on the mother ship any more than I helped my friends in Canada before the UFN nuclear strike," he said. "I can't help you, my friends." Jason sat on the plains of Himachal Pradesh and put his head in his hands.

The ModuCom's external speakers rocked with the sound of explosions.

Blue-white bolts of light flashed inside the mother ship. One captain, who stood at the general's side, was killed when a laser beam bounced against a wall.

Queen Taranta screamed in her cell. A tower of honeycomb was sliced in half and melted. Soft furry bodies imploded around her.

"Little pet, help us," Zibb called. "The farthest rooms in the ship are burning. Sections of metal are breaking off and falling to—"

Crackle...

"Zibb?" Their connection was breaking up. "Pakistan, China, Tibet are covered with pieces of the ship."

"Little pet, I'm dying."

"No!"

Escape pods, filled with workers and drones, fell smoking to the ground. Loyal wasps swarmed their battle stations, to be stuck through by columns of metal. General Vard threw his barbs into the air and putrid poison spattered the metal walls in the control room.

"I'll stand my ground." The death ray pulsed into space. Jason could hear the general's words.

"General Vard aimed the death ray at the inside of his own ship to stop our rebellion, turned against his own kind," Zibb said through the red box.

The general then seemed to remember the new queen and his duty to her. "Taranta," he buzzed. "You're in peril. Our mission is in danger—my wasps, my queen, and our disloyal subjects riding the mother ship to their death. I'm sorry, Your Highness. In my rage, I destroyed us all. But you're not the leader you should have been."

The ship was no longer impenetrable, no longer safe refuge as its shields buckled and tore.

"I'm disappointed in my queen." General Vard clenched his jaw. "You seemed so nice and warlike at home, and now you only sit with the nurses and eat royal jelly and honeycomb, wiggle your belly to the newest music and allow yourself to be entertained by that little pet of the worker bee, Zitt, or was it Zidd? Something like that."

Zibb grinned.

The general continued. "What was the human's name? Jellyroll? Justice? Oh, Jason. And the worker, Zibb." General Vard grabbed his head as if it hurt.

The huge mother ship shook apart and fell from the sky over India, its screens not working. "We're full of traitors and a strange human army on board."

"A house turned against itself cannot stand," Jason remembered, watching the flaming display and the huge mother ship breaking up over the plains.

The mother ship continued to fall, debris clanging to Earth, explosions rocking the decks.

"General," shouted the second lieutenant at the bank of controls. "We're going to crash."

"Stupid fools!" The general flung his poison barbs at the neck of a nearby sergeant. "Raise the shields. Power up!"

"Impossible, sir," a group of soldiers said. Their barbed claws raced over the control panels. "By heaven, sir, the workers are still dancing!"

So they were. A death dance perhaps, but a dance still, they buzzed and jumped around the huge broken rooms of the sky-ship, which stretched for miles, a dance of happy freedom and victory in the grip of terror.

Zibb's translator in the hold of the ship had not been destroyed. Jason's music swelled.

Quiet that damnable racket! General Vard went back to quantum thought like their ancestors, like the small earth bees who were telepathic. Zibb and her cousins moved closer to Queen

Taranta as the great ship limped to Earth, its magnetic field braking their fall. Workers tore themselves from their stations, from their feeding tubes, from their dances and rode their burning home to the top of the Himalayas.

The ship perched like an ark on *Ama Dablam*, the "Mother and Her Necklace," in Nepal. Scores of escape pods dotted the landscape as far away as Mongolia and the borders of Russia.

"We'll find a palace for you," General Vard promised as the queen's soldiers placed the queen and the nurses in a gleaming escape pod.

"Go with her, Zibb," Banter urged. The Black Watch didn't see Zibb as she slipped in beside the queen. The Pod's jets flamed as the small craft rose into the air and flew toward China.

"Goodbye, General Vard." The queen wiggled a white arm. "Don't worry about us. We'll be all right."

"Farewell, your majesty. You're the least of my worries."

"You're safe, my queen," Zibb said from the pod. "That's all that counts. You must hold your people together spiritually."

"We don't believe in spirituality," a young nurse reminded her.

"God save the queen," Zibb saluted. Zibb was a monarchist to the core.

Slowly the SpaceHive tipped from the mountaintop to the valleys below. The great ship crashed, buckled and burned. The wasp general remained in what was left of the ship, true to his duty.

"Come to Nepal, all you thousands of airships in the skies of the new Jive Hive, in the skies of Earth. Come to Nepal and help us," General Vard called on all speakers from what remained of the control room in the SpaceHive.

The Dutch airships limped back to their headquarters in Uttar Pradesh to regroup. Jason was shaken but unhurt on the plain. The pod containing the queen continued to China.

"Zibb?" His PAD was silent. "Zibb, my friend, come in."

Silence.

In Himachal Pradesh, the humans came together again, seeing the fate of the huge mother ship. Jason's music soared over the plains, over the airwaves to aliens, the bees. Scores of human soldiers poured across the border from Pakistan.

Zibb flew with Queen Taranta and the nurses over the Himalayas.

"The queen is in China." Zibb's barbed hands grasped the red translator.

"Zibb, you're with the queen?"

"I can't talk anymore, little pet."

"We're losing power, Zibb. Stay there. I'll be in touch."

Back in India, General Vard stood his ground and snarled.

"Show them mercy," Zibb said.

"Mercy? They'll take it as a sign of weakness. We must kill them all."

The Dutch commander brought his forces together again. He knew the battle was not over until every alien ship had been destroyed. The Austrians poured across the border in their megacopters with bombs and laser cannons.

Jason's ZipPAD was quiet. Far away, in the hills, Aadab hugged his girlfriend. He had found Iodine wandering the paths in front of his cave.

"My Canadian friend had a dream." Aadab held butter-yellow mountain flowers in his hands for his girl. "He had a dream of Shiva. Your god, Iodine. Not mine. But he dreamed of the name of Allah, too. Allah be praised. It was a sign."

"Shiva and other gods we worship in this time of victory and joy," Iodine said in Hindi. "God be praised."

"Did the wasps survive?" Aadab thumbed the SmartPAD. "The mother ship is gone, broken apart on the mountain. What of the wasp general and the alien soldiers? What of our friends in the ranks of the aliens?"

No answer from Jason.

The earth would eventually fall if any alien wasps remained.

Jason, in his place in the Rajgarh Valley, wiped sweat from his eyes and chose another song. He thought of his scientist father and librarian mother, his new brother—he had a strong feeling the baby was going to be a boy—and Bill Glass in Yahk with his dog, Freedom.

What was the joke Mr. Glass liked to tell about his dog?

"I went to a justice of the peace when I got married," he'd told Jason a while ago, "and asked if I could have Freedom at my wedding. I said, 'I had Freedom before I was married.' The JP said, 'No, this isn't the place for it. You'll have to wait until after the wedding.' I said, 'You don't understand. She's a dog.' The J.P. said, 'I don't care how she looks. You can't have freedom at your wedding.'"

Jason grinned. He missed Mr. Glass. He missed his friends, his family, the normal life he'd lived in Creston, British Columbia, before the bees and wasps changed everything.

"You're a hero, Jason. You there? Your music saved the world. Smart move, l'il Canadian."

"No, we haven't saved the world, Aadab. Not yet. There's an answer somewhere, a secret my father knew. My father. My mother."

"Both dead, my friend?"

"I'm afraid so, Aadab. But there's something he said once, what was it?"

Jason saw the mighty ship explode, scattering into smoking pieces of metal over the plains. Escape pods crackled through the air like fireworks.

"Thank goodness that Zibb is in China with the queen. Queen Taranta is in China. The royal jelly! That's the secret!"

He struck his forehead with the back of his hand. "I've been so stupid, Aadab!"

"No, not you, Jay."

"We've got to get to China. We have to find the queen and Zibb. How fast can you get here? You know how to find me, pal, from the numbers on your PAD. Place Iodine somewhere safe and come and get me. Quickly, Aadab."

"You got it, Jason. What are you thinking?"

"I'll tell you when you get here."

Chapter Fifteen

Jason tuned his ZipPAD to the broadcast from Haridwar. Still the same. "The President of the United States, Maria Black, KY3 calling. We ask for your help. Is anyone there? Read me. Is anyone there? Antarctica, Station Blue calling."

"Yes, we are here, Antarctica Blue. This is Jason Anderson."

There was a pause. "Who are you?"

Static on the air, then a man's voice."Jay? President Black, with all respect. This is Steve Anderson. Is my son on the uberline? Please."

"Dad?"

"Oh my. What a shock. Like a dream come true. I'm so proud and relieved. Are you all right? What happened to you, Jay?"

"I'm fine. I'm in India with a friend and fellow freedom fighter. The old channel still works, Dad. Can't believe it's you."

"You must have a heck of a story, Son. Change channels as soon as you can. I have a surprise for you."

"I'm on my way to China. SpaceHive has been destroyed. Repeat, the mother ship has been destroyed. The black general may still be alive, but the European Union is now in control. However, much of Earth ruined. Much loss of life." Jason paused, thinking about his mother. "Dad? About Mom..."

"We'll talk in a bit, Jason. There's someone here who needs to speak with you."

There was a pause and then a female voice. "Maria Black here."

"President Black?" Jason's mouth hung open in disbelief. He was talking with the president of the United States.

"Yes, Jason. I understand you have information for us. What do we need to do?"

"Get your airships together, if you can," he said. "And your best soldiers and a couple of scientists. Send them to India. Talk to the research labs there in Station Blue and tell them to wrap up the work on the Andromeda protein that my father was working on a year ago."

"I think he's almost finished his work on it," she said. "Why is it so important?"

"Eating royal jelly can cause death in people allergic to bee or wasp venom. We're going to make sure it's made into poison to the aliens. My father was working on a protein to turn their own royal food against them. I think he was onto something."

"Yes, he's talked about it."

"Our bodies are different. We can turn the tables and make the royal jelly deadly for the queen, who needs it to survive. Queenless, all the aliens, including the Black Watch, will lose direction and die."

A voice interrupted from Antarctica, a man's face on the little Zip monitor coming into view. "My name's Joseph Zeller. I'm the Chief of Defense here at the UFN. From what I understand this queen doesn't count for much. It's the wasps we must worry about."

"The wasps follow their queen. It's a biological fact. I've observed it in colonies of bees," Jason said.

"I must consult my experts," President Black interrupted. "We'll be in touch."

"No time. Get all your biochemists working on that Andromeda protein, and tell my father to lead. Then get your people up here please, President. We must give it to all the wasps as soon as we can."

"Why? The war appears to be over. The mother ship is down. The airships all came to India and went down with the mother ship."

He wiped his face with a dirty hand. "I believe the wasps are still alive, still in what's left of the mother ship or in pods that fell over India. The smaller alien ships that remain are now getting ready for a second wave of attacks."

"The Black Watch? The black general? Where are they?"

"They went down with their mother ship, now scattered in smoking pieces on the sides of the mountain. We don't know for sure if the alien general was killed when his ship went down. If he's alive, then in his rage he could still be an awesome force against us."

"Do you know the whereabouts of their queen?" Zeller asked.

"Yes. She's in China, and my friend is with her."

"Your friend?"

"It's a long story. Her name is Zibb."

"An alien?"

"Yes, but she is kind. And a bee, not a wasp."

"Wait." Zeller's image disappeared and his father's face filled the small screen.

"Dad?" Jason said.

"Your mother will be so proud."

"*Will* be? Mom's alive?"

"Yes," his father said. "We've been in touch over a different channel. Somehow it's cleared enough to get through the interference around the nuclear site. She's still in the bunker at Kamloops. But we've found a way to stop the radioactive ash that lies over North America."

"Can you patch me through to her, Dad?"

"I can try."

His mother's voice, faint yet so sweet, reached his ears. "Jason."

"I'm here, Mom. I'm so glad you're okay. I was so scared."

"I know, honey. But we're all okay. Even the baby."

Jason's eyes blurred with tears. His family was safe.

I am not alone.

After speaking with his parents for a few more minutes, Jason ran back into the forest below Ama Dablam, in the midst of fragments from the SpaceHive. There he saw the air scooter limping from the direction of Uttar Pradesh.

The air scooter set down on the grass a few yards from Jason.

"Aadab," he called, waving. "Glad to see you."

Aadab was holding Iodine's hand and made no move to take off.

"We gotta go," Jason said as he punched controls on his Zip-PAD.

"Go where?" Aadab asked. "Why are we in a hurry? We won."

"My friend needs our help. Zibb is with the alien queen. She holds the secret."

"What secret?"

"Later. Let's go." Jason twisted his palm on the PAD and music poured from the speakers. "I hope this music reaches Zibb and Queen Taranta, to work its magic and stop the spell of the monarch."

"The queen is still alive?" Aadab asked, increasing the speed of the air scooter.

Jason nodded. "She's all that remains of the influence of General Vard and his Black Watch, and she's a formidable force. We know some of the Black Watch escaped in pods too, and they'll still be a threat to Earth. The allied forces must destroy the last of these aliens."

"Except your friend Zibb."

"Yeah," Jason said. "And a few other bees. Zibb can tell us who is friend or enemy. But all the wasps that follow General Vard must die. The Black Watch soldiers that escaped in the pods are probably sick and exhausted."

Aadab frowned. "Where do you think they went?"

"Some may be in China, looking for their queen. We must take the royal jelly from the bees and from Queen Taranta, leaving her helpless. Her wasps will be unable to fight. The queen is in the open now, not safe anymore in the mother ship. We must strike now, strip the hives of nectar and honeycomb, smoke out the bees, turn the music up. Jazz, rap, rock and roll."

"We'll win this battle," Aadab said, patting Jason on the shoulder.

Jason paused for a moment, then said, "The royal jelly is surely the key. Why didn't I think of it before? It fed Queen Taranta and kept her alive, and the queen kept the aliens together. Queen Taranta must die. What's left of the wasps must be killed or they'll band together and destroy us another day.

"How we going to do that, my friend?"

"With my father's research, the serum he prepared and the royal jelly."

"Climb up front and change places with Iodine," Aadab said. "We'll go as far as we can get to China. It's just over the border from Tibet."

Jason exchanged seats with Iodine. "Will this thing make it that far?"

Aadab laughed. "It'll make it to the moon and back." At Jason's surprised expression, he snorted. "That was a joke. But it'll make it to China."

When they got to the mountains in the north of India, Aadab lowered the air scooter to the ground and Iodine climbed down.

"I'll be back for you," Aadab promised. "Keep warm and safe."

"I know there are air scooters here in the mountains," Iodine said. "And other people hiding from the war. I'm a big girl, Aadab. I'll meet you at the border when this is all over."

"Not with the Chinese guards. Not safe. Meet us in Burma. That's a neutral place right now. I'll join you there. I promise."

Waving goodbye to Iodine, Aadab lifted the scooter into the air and off they flew. They flew over streams and forests, mountains and lakes. Some areas had been destroyed by fire.

Jason was a bit nervous at first, but soon was able to relax.

Flying in an air scooter isn't so bad.

He thought of Zibb. Would they get there in time to save her? And stop the queen and the remainder of her army?

They landed on the plains near the mountain ranges to the west of the Tibetan Plateau, their airship out of fuel. China sprawled beyond to the east, yet they couldn't go any farther in the crippled air scooter.

"China is huge," Aadab said. "And the people are very smart. They will help us."

"I'm counting on it. But why didn't they help the African and European allies? The Russians were there and helped us. Where were the Asians?"

"The Chinese were working on something to escape. I heard it through a Chinese freedom fighter. Soldiers like me, we know everything." Aadab laughed. "They've been working on gigantic flying arks to escape Earth. The ark ships will carry thousands of people. They call them Star Shelters."

"We won't need a ship. Too late for that. But we do need their help."

Jason stretched his long legs in the seat beside Aadab, spoke into the voice controls and the doors opened onto the slopes and plains of Tibet. In the distance they could see the long border of China. Asian soldiers were moving toward them in open Jeeps.

Just then the air scooter spoke. *"Fuel empty. Fuel empty."*

"Uh-oh," Jason said.

Chapter Sixteen

The Asian soldiers rolled in their open military trucks from the border point into Tibet. They all stood around Aadab and Jason. A sergeant dressed in a camo uniform stepped forward and spoke in good English.

"What are you doing here?" the sergeant asked. "So close to our border? As you know, we claim Tibet as well. No one is allowed to go beyond the Tibetan plains."

"There has been a great war," Jason said. "The mother ship is destroyed. The alien queen has fled into China."

"We know about the battle," the sergeant said. "We listened to the European CyberPADs. Many airships have crashed into our country, and some have been shot down."

"China is a great country," Aadab said, "the greatest country in the world, next to mine. Why didn't you join us in our war?"

"That's a state matter. We have millions of people in the hills to protect. We can't go beyond our borders to fight for other armies."

"Your cities were destroyed and with them much of your military?"

"Oh, no," the Asian said. "Our military remains thousands strong with mighty men and women of the state. We're saving our strength for the final day."

"We now know the aliens left the hills and air space over the rest of the world to help the wasp leaders, who fled from the mother ship when it was destroyed by the European forces. China, too, has alien escape pods, and we're coming to look for one," Jason said.

The Asian soldier coughed. "We heard all about it on our CyberPADS. Our military is camped along the borders here, along the Democratic Republics of Vietnam, Tibet, Kazakhstan, Pakistan, India, Russia, United Korea and the Pacific Ocean. We allow no one to come or go. We know about the enemy's pods escaping into our valleys and mountains and the hives they try to build. We think the queen was with one of them."

"Why didn't you join the European Union and the rest of the world in the Dutch attack?" Aadab Ali asked again.

"China has her own plans," the soldier muttered.

The soldiers stepped forward with laser guns and K-13s slung across their shoulders.

Jason stroked the side of the downed air scooter. "We're out of solar fuel. Can you help us?"

One of the soldiers stepped forward. "What's your name?"

Jason told him and introduced his friend as well, both as freedom fighters.

Another Chinese soldier strode up. She saluted. "Please, sir? May I speak?"

"Of course," the sergeant said. "What do you have to say, soldier?"

"I've heard this boy spoken of in the ranks. He is a friend of the aliens. Maybe a spy."

"Yes?"

The soldier hefted a gun and pointed it at Jason, while the rest of the unit covered Aadab with their light laser guns. Another soldier reached into the air scooter and tapped on the fuel gauge panel, which responded in a hollow tone, "Empty. Empty."

"No fuel, sir. We'll take their weapons."

"Very well." The sergeant swung his rifle toward the pair. "Come with me."

A cold wind blew from the mountain range onto the Tibetan plain. The sergeant looked at the sky where escape pods still flared across the border, many shot down by Chinese border guards with their Nanking Cherry 200 missiles.

"We have our own plans." The Asian sergeant loaded the weapons from the crippled airship and Aadab's few things into the back of the Jeep.

"You're building a Star Shelter," Aadab said. "I heard about it— ships to take men and women to the Antarctic, then into space."

The Jeeps purred to life and made their way back to the border. Jason swayed in the cramped seat beside the sergeant. Aadab hunched beside an armed soldier in the cargo space in the back.

"You seem to know a lot," the soldier said, eyeing Aadab with suspicion.

Aadab shrugged. "Not so much."

The sergeant took the safety bar off his laser gun. "We think you're spies."

Aadab shook his head. "No. We're not spies. We heard you're building spaceships to move people off the earth."

"Who told you that?" the sergeant demanded.

"It's all over the air waves. Freedom fighters around the world know what you're doing."

"We're fighting the same enemy," Jason piped up. "I was a prisoner in the mother ship for many months in Canada—until their site was bombed."

"That was a big mistake," the sergeant said. "Radioactive dust is everywhere now."

"We all die," the soldier said, "or we live together in peace."

"Yes," Jason agreed. "But didn't you hear that scientists in Antarctica discovered a way to clear the radioactive dust?"

"I didn't hear that. If you are a spy, you'll be very sorry, boy."

"I'm not a spy. And this fellow behind me is a freedom fighter from India. We're united against an alien world, together for the first time in history. Join us."

"China will win the war," the sergeant said.

Border shacks loomed with the missile fields in the background, protected by electric fences.

"China is a great nation," Aadab said with a smile. "But we are all one great nation, this Earth."

"Yes," the soldier said. "If you say it is."

The truck hummed to a stop.

Guards pulled Jason from his seat.

"Hey!" Aadab said. "Leave him alone. He's just a kid."

"You are trespassing," one of the guards said.

"This is Jason Anderson," the sergeant said. "He may be a spy."

"For the bees?"

The small soldier held up her rifle. "The bees love him."

"*Traitor*," the border guard spat. "Move!"

"And who are you?" the guard asked Aadab, who was standing beside the Jeep.

"I'm a freedom fighter from Uttar Pradesh in India. This boy is not a spy. We're friends. I count my life on his loyalty to Earth."

"You may both stay in our jails for a long time until this is proven." the guard said, tying Jason's hands behind him with metal twists. "Come. We'll take you both to the captain."

He stumbled toward the biggest border shack. Zibb was here in China somewhere, sure to be in touch again. The Asians thought Jason was a spy because of his friendship with the alien bee. How could he prove he wasn't a spy?

Jason groaned as the guard took away his ZipPAD. "Do you understand your mistake? You're helping the enemy by keeping us prisoners." He saw the huge holograph screen inside the hut blazing with many numbers and maps. It was dimmed at a command from the man seated in front of it, but not before Jason had taken in the details of the huge Star Shelters and their specs.

The man who sat in front of the screen was explaining something, in Chinese, to the military.

"This is a very important engineer," the sergeant explained. "He also speaks okay English."

The engineer rubbed his forehead. "What are they doing here? I'm very busy, soldier."

"Sorry, sir," the soldier said. "Military orders, directly from the captain. They were to be brought here."

"Not here. Surely you're in the wrong place, Sergeant. Don't you know this is top secret?"

"Why is an engineer working at a border crossing?" Jason asked.

"Because it's all they have left of their military," Aadab said. "Isn't it?" He turned to a man with a captain's badge. The captain was biting his nails in a corner of the room, hunched in front of another wall screen.

The same soldier they had met earlier entered the room with a laser gun in her hands. "Sir, this is a spy."

"Thank you, soldier," the captain said. "You may have a break now."

"As a friend who knows the enemy, you can help us," the captain said. "Or..."

"Or we go to jail?" Jason asked. "You don't have to threaten us. I'd be glad to help."

"The rest of the world will help us?" the captain asked, as the engineer began making notes on a puter-terminal.

"The rest of the world is with China," Jason said. "We would have been one world on the Star Shelters. Isn't that right? Would *you* leave your friends behind?"

"Star Shelters?" The engineer tapped his fingers on the desk. "Ah, yes."

"Star Shelters," the captain said. "Earth's last line of defense, wouldn't you agree?"

Where was Zibb now? And Queen Taranta?

"Could you really have moved the remaining world's population to the last safe base on Earth, or off the planet—and would you have done that?"

"You say the world won't need to move into space now?" the Asian captain asked.

"Earth will win if they finish my father's formula that would turn the aliens' own venom against the queen and wasps."

"Really? We are interested. Tell me more."

"My father also knows the serum could be used on humans to cure diseases and extend life. It would take only a few tweaks of the formula to do that."

"This is your father's hope and dream, and yours too? How amusing." The captain winked at the engineer and swept his arm across the puterhologram to show off the Star Ship plans. "We have much a better plan than that."

"Don't show them our plans," the engineer said. "Too much risk when they are traitors, sir."

"Yes." The captain turned off the screen.

Jason thought of Zibb and how he planned to rescue her. "Am I a traitor because I didn't kill a friendly alien? That's a compliment, sir."

"Your family will never see you again," the captain threatened.

Jason thought of his mother, whose voice had been rough when she spoke on their shared channel. She'd seemed stunned and overwhelmed to have proof that he was alive. Was she shattered with joy to know she had not lost her first-born son?

I love my mother and father. And the brother I have not yet met.

Now he had something to live for. His family had survived.

He glanced at the Chinese soldiers. It didn't matter what they thought. He knew he was no traitor. And one day they'd know that too.

Jason smiled. *I'll find a way to save the world.*

Chapter Seventeen

Outside the Chinese border hut a cold wind howled. A Nanking Cherry 200 missile blasted into the air. Jason watched it streak across the sky, praying that it would not kill any innocent people.

Aadab watched too, his eyes filled with fear.

The Asian captain jabbed Aadab, then poked his finger at the holograph screen. "Our chief engineer thinks you can help. There is a little problem here with our plans." The captain hunched in front of the blueprints.

Aadab peered over the man's shoulder. "That's the design of the Star Shelter? There is a—"

"What do you know, Indian boy?" the captain interrupted.

"I know much about electronics. I know computers well, even as a small boy."

"Too young to be well trained. Maybe we just shoot you both."

"I was trained in general science," Aadab said. "Trained in New Delhi and graduated from upper school with honors. My relatives gave up much to send me to a good university. They wanted me to learn English well, become a citizen of the world. I would have PhD if the war hadn't happened first. I have the *best* training."

The captain scowled. "What do you know about China?"

"I go to uber-modern school." Aadab grinned. "I watch stere-ocam all the time. I learn a lot about rest of world and learned from good teachers from all over world."

"Did you learn engineering?"

"Yes."

"My friend is a great engineer," Jason said.

The captain shrugged. "Can help us, maybe. We introduce you to our engineer in charge."

Aadab nodded. "I am no spy, I promise you."

"We shall see. Where you work?"

"In town of Haridwar. I ran their electricity, their power grids and their solar nuclear panels all alone. I set up power again after town was destroyed."

The captain paced the room for a moment. "I'm Captain Lin Ming-Hoa. Your name?"

"I am Aadab Ali. This is Jason Anderson, my friend, no traitor."

"You both are very valuable if you not spies," the captain said. "My soldiers say you are spies."

"Check with the European Union," Jason said. "They'll tell you I felled the mother ship with the help of a—"

"Bee?" Captain Lin finished the sentence.

"Well, yes."

"Bee your friend?"

"It's like this—"

"You can use engineer and smart boy?" Aadab spoke up. "My friend was prisoner of bees and wasps for many months. Learned much. Destroyed their big airship, is planning to destroy all of wasps now, followed queen into China. We have plan to destroy wasps, destroy queen."

"Really?" Captain Lin sat down next to Jason. "Ah, my friend. You not spy?"

"I'll help you. I know more about the bees than anyone on Earth."

"Oh. Very good, Anderson Jason."

"Allah is the greatest," Aadab said. He put his hands together and bowing his head, faced what he hoped was the historic Mecca.

"Pray then." The captain shrugged. "We need prayer."

"Why?" Jason asked. "Because this is all that's left of your army?"

"Millions of soldiers." The engineer waved his hand in several directions. "Out there." He turned his attention to the hologram screen again.

"Patch me through to Dutch general," Captain Lin said to the sergeant, who began to thumb the controls of a military StarPAD.

"I understand Star Shelter," Aadab added after finishing his prayers.

"Oh, do you?" The engineer ran a hand through his glossy hair. "We have a small problem."

"Yes." Aadab got up and jabbed at the wall screen with his index finger. "Right here. Flaw in design."

"Yes. I know. Can't fix."

"Yes." Aadab took a stylus from the desk and began to scribble over the surface of the notebook, numbers dancing in air.

"Ah," Captain Lin spoke into the StarPAD. He listened and smiled. "Very good."

Another soldier entered the hut and whispered something to the sergeant.

"Outside our borders," the sergeant reported. "There is trouble."

"Trouble?" Jason asked, as missiles exploded into the evening sky.

"The Black Watch attack in small airships, using death rays and heat guns. They not dead yet. Alien general not dead. Learn all this from own source in hills."

"Sounds right. The general's a tough old wasp."

99

"I call Dutch general, like this Canadian boy suggested, talk to him for short time, make sure it is right guy, Sergeant. I ask him about these two fellows."

"What did the Dutch General say?"

"He say boy not traitor. He is genius. His music destroyed SpaceHive."

"Music?" The sergeant's eyes widened.

"Music," Jason said with a nod. "A little weapon I learned about from my friend on the ship."

"The bee?"

"Yes. They're not all bad, you know. Some just want to be free."

"And dance," Aadab said.

"Free and dance?" Captain Lin swept his arm toward the stark landscape outside the little window. "We all want that."

"The alien queen is in China. You must help us find her."

"Why we should help you two boys?"

"Because I know how to destroy her, and when she's gone, the bees will be tame like kites without a wind." Jason got up and walked to the hologram screen. "The bees will group around her if she remains alive, and the wasps will also group around their queen. We must help them live in peace—without their dark friends, without the warlike queen and her friend General Vard and his army."

"Help the bees? You are traitor."

"No," Aadab said. "He knows the truth. He knows some bees are good bees."

"No good bees. They destroyed our country. We will fight and then flee to Antarctica, then to space in Star Shelters we build here in China."

"The Black Watch will find you again. They have spaceships. We must stay and defeat the wasps, defeat the queen, defeat evil and help the good bees. The good ones will help us, too. The earth is already greener in many places. It can be a paradise."

"No good bees. You traitor." The soldier moved closer to Jason, a hand on her ack ack.

"You talked to the Dutch general." Jason spread his hands wide. "He told you the truth."

"Maybe Anderson Jason fool Dutch general. Dutch commander maybe not know."

"He was there when the mother ship crashed. I tell you, you must give me back my ZipPAD. It's programmed with music that brought down the bees. They respond to music. The vibes make them remember how to dance. Something—I don't know what—but something in the music calms them. Tames them. I noticed it when they first took me prisoner. There was a bee who heard my music when I first met her. She became my friend. I noticed how she got so calm when she heard the music. I remembered that and used it on the rest of the wasps and bees. It worked."

"Music? You are very strange boy, Anderson."

Jason straightened and lifted his chin. "The world has got to work *together*. You can't destroy the world because you don't trust me. What did the Dutchman say?"

"Dutch general says you are hero. We shall see." He turned to the sergeant. "Return this boy's PAD to him."

Jason grabbed the ZipPad and handed it to Aadab.

Aadab eyed the engineer. "Now, do you want my help?"

The Asian man shrugged.

"You have room for everyone," Aadab's hands flew over the controls, "if you do this and this." He suggested different ways of making the Star Ship design better. "I am only a young fellow, twenty years old, but I am one smart cookie."

"You are one smart cookie." Jason grinned and clutched his ZipPAD. He spoke into the controls.

Was his friend Zibb alive? Would she be there when he needed her?

The PAD remained silent. "Is there any food in this place?" Jason turned to the captain. "I'm hungry."

"We have rations."

"I'm not used to anything better than soldiers' rations." A voice took form in his mind. *Are you there, little pet?* A weak voice. *So hungry. Queen ate all food in the pod. Nothing left.*

"Zibb!" He cried into his PAD. "Where are you?" *Traitor,* he thought. *Traitor. This is your friend, Zibb. And you, Jason Anderson, are a traitor to your friend. But not a traitor to the human race. The queen must die.* "Yes, Zibb. I am here. I have food for you all. But you will have to wait a few days."

Where is food?

"You are hurt, Zibb? You can't gather honeycomb and fruit where you crashed?"

I am hurt. It is hard to move my arms.

"I will have food for you all. Food from Antarctica. Honeycomb and royal jelly. For Queen Taranta."

And me?

"Yes. For you, Zibb. Special royal jelly. Just hang on, and we'll help you." *Traitor.*

Was help on the way from Antarctica? Was his father's Andromeda protein packed and ready to go? Would it work?

Would it kill the queen?

What? Zibb whispered.

"Nothing."

He turned the music up. The Four Black Skulls played loud and fast, and Jason pictured the drums setting a small alien group to dancing in their crashed pod on a mountaintop in China. He imagined an alien queen sinking her barbs into the neck of her nearest nurse.

"Zibb?"

Silence.

I'm a traitor. He hung his head.

The weak connection was broken and he turned to Captain Lin. "I'm expecting the Americans any day now. Let them in across your borders. They have a special serum my father's been working on for many months. It's a sort of poison, sir, and it will poison their queen."

"Without the queen they will fail?"

"Either that or we'll poison the whole bunch." Jason clenched his jaw. "All of them. And we'll get the black general for sure, somehow. Some way. The general should have died ten times over when the mother ship crashed, but our sources say he lived."

The Americans arrived the next morning on a Japanese Thunderbear II jet fighter, with the modified royal jelly and the Andromeda protein in the back. Would Jason's plot work? Would the Asians be able to put his plan into place without the queen or wasps knowing what they planned?

Zibb. I'm sorry.

The American scientists left their awesome cargo there on the borders of China. They brought with them weapons from Antarctica, including a scope gun capable of loading a charge of Proto-Xybramine strong enough to kill a wasp on contact. A pilot and two military guards returned with them to New Delhi, where they joined the European forces. They left the Chinese to take the poison to the queen.

"Ah, sacred Taoist mountain," Captain Lin said on hearing of the place where the queen's pod had gone down. "Pines and cypresses below there, maybe rock temples, no food for the bees. Good."

"This is special royal jelly," Jason said to the Asian soldiers. "It must be moved carefully. The honey too, mixed with the special protein our allies have made in Antarctica. My father's work was almost finished when I was taken prisoner by the bee. Now it is complete."

"Hope it works, man," Aadab said. "Those bees said they are hungry?"

"Yes. They've eaten all their food and can't find any more in that rocky place, and with their injuries. This food should put them into a strong allergic shock, and I'm hoping the queen will die. There's a sort of telepathy among them. I hope it doesn't alert them to the danger."

The Asian rocket plane left at noon, following a trace to the mountain where Queen Taranta's pod had crashed. With them they brought their deadly goods. Jason heard a few hours later that the poisoned food had been dropped to the queen's pod where Zibb and the nurses also were starving. For sure they would eat without question.

Traitor. Jason's brain thundered, and this time he felt like crying for the death of his friend and their friendship. Zibb would surely die because of the food he supplied.

Chapter Eighteen

"Thank you for the food." The PAD broadcast Zibb's gratitude.

Jason wiped tears from his eyes. "Give it to Queen Taranta first." Zibb must trust him. And he would trust his apian friend.

"Listen to me, Zibb, my friend. *Don't eat the food.*" He sensed Zibb's surprise.

Zibb had helped him and humanity. She was Jason's good friend. "Don't eat the royal jelly or the honey. Don't eat it, Zibb. Feed it to the queen. Let the nurses eat it. Leave it for the wasps. Don't touch it yourself."

Captain Lin reached for the ZipPAD, trying to turn it off. Jason tore himself away and ran outside into the mist.

"What is it, little pet? The food is here. We offer it first to the queen. She is starving."

"Yes! Feed the queen, Zibb. But don't eat it yourself."

"Why not?"

"You must trust me, Zibb. I'm coming. Hold on!"

"Hold on? We are injured, all of us. And some died in the crash. We have eaten the dead. Now there's no food left, only pine and cypress forests below here and rock."

"You know what to do, Zibb. Turn your speakers to full volume. I'll send music. It will ease the pain."

"Pain?"

"Oh, you are so innocent, my friend."

Silence.

Then a high-pitched, venomous voice asked, "Earthling?" Queen Taranta continued. "Is something wrong with this package of food your airship has dropped off for us?"

"No."

"Why would you help us, white-faced, nude-skinned fodder?"

Silence.

Jason tuned his ZipPAD incoming posts to *Sleep*. He began to broadcast Total Chaos Boys and Electric Sunday, the trumpets and strings rising at the base of the bees' hearing levels and higher, where he could not hear them soar into the air of Taishan far to the east in Shandong Province.

It would take Jason, the pilot and the Asian guards many hours to get there in a large megacopter to airlift the dying or dead aliens, if Captain Lin would agree.

Jason knew the area from a glance at the hologram screen in the hut behind him. Aadab had rigged the controls to show the region where he knew Queen Taranta, her nurses and Zibb had landed.

"The sacred mountain," Jason told the captain. "The pod crashed near a stone temple with images of dead dynasties carved in the rock. It would be hard to airlift any survivors out of there. They would have to be moved carefully."

"And if the queen and her nurses have been killed by the poison?"

"With Taranta gone, there'll be chaos. Queenless, the wasps will no longer be able to rule. Their life's mission to lead would end with the death of their leader. The Black Watch looked to the queen for their unity."

"But how we kill them?"

"We won't have to. They'll be starving. They'll feed on their dead queen and her nurses."

"Ah...the poison will kill them too."

"Exactly." Jason paused for a moment. "But from my understanding of their culture, I think the Black Watch could still be a threat."

"How?"

"They may be too smart to eat. They may smell the poison. I don't know. I don't know enough about their species." Jason frowned. "And I don't know enough about the young queen they brought with them on their long journey to Earth. Without her, the alien general will have trouble controlling the rest of his troops, and especially the gentle worker bees, nurses and drones."

"Hope your plan works, boy."

"Let's hope Taranta ate the poison and after her, the wasps too. We'll leave a trap for them. If the queen doesn't warn them first before she dies. *If* she dies. Captain, this is a long shot." Jason put his head in his hands.

Aadab stood beside him.

"What?" Jason heard the crackle of the translator over the airwaves. His PAD whispered to life. Brahms's Third Symphony. Their song.

"Zibb! I'm glad you called me back. Thanks for trusting me. How are the queen and her nurses? Have they eaten?"

"Queen Taranta is dead, and the nurses also have eaten." Zibb sounded defeated and sad. "You warned me, friend, but I almost wish I could join my queen in death."

Captain Lin passed by just at that moment. Hearing the alien transmission, he let out a yell and ripped the ZipPAD from Jason's fingers. "You are a traitor, Anderson Jason. I knew it! You cannot be trusted. You're warning the traitor. Death to all aliens and traitors. There shouldn't be one left alive. She'll alert the general and his wasps."

"Zibb is a friend. She only wants peace. Just like we all do. She's a bee, not a wasp."

The captain grunted. "Bees, wasps—they're all the same."

"But they're not all the same," Jason said.

"China's bright cities are *gone*," the captain snapped. "We look to a boy for help, a boy who might be a traitor. But if the worst happens, we still have the Star Shelters, built with China's best minds. We will escape and live to fight again after a long time in space, perhaps on a friendly planet far away. We have great minds. We know how to survive."

"I can be faithful to both my friends and the world." Jason reached out a hand for the ZipPAD. "Give it to me. I know what to do."

"You've done it. You've alerted the enemy. Guards, seize him."

"No! The music is still playing over the speakers. It will lull them."

"And the queen ate the poison," Aadab assured the captain.

The captain ignored Aadab and grabbed Jason by the shoulders. "One of the aliens has been alerted. You are either stupid or a traitor."

"I trust in our friendship. The bee loves me."

"Love," the captain scoffed. "The bee is an alien. You are her pet. You have betrayed your country?"

"I didn't betray my country," Jason yelled. "Or my world. Give me back the PAD, sir. I swear the queen is dead if my friend Zibb says she is."

"You *did* betray your world," the soldier who'd been watching them said. "I ask that you let me shoot him, sir."

"No!" Aadab cried. "Jason is only a boy. He is good person. He has mother and father, still alive. Baby brother. Jason is protected by Allah. Allah is great. *Allahu akbar.*"

The captain left the room for a moment. Jason and Aadab just stared at each other, wondering about their fate.

When the captain returned, he said, "I have no choice. I have to believe my own species. I believe you, Urdu man. I believe Anderson is a good boy. Dutch general also said he is good." He grabbed Jason's arm, gently this time. "Let's go, lover of bees. We airlift your friend and dead queen back to be incinerated."

"You believe me now?" Jason asked.

"I believe your Indian friend." He nodded to a soldier to escort Aadab.

Jason mouthed *'thank you'* to Aadab.

"I must trust you both and Dutch general," the captain continued. "We should not fight one another. We must stand united. Fight enemy."

"Where are we going?" Jason asked.

"We leave now to find your bee friend—and the dead queen. The Americans vouch for you, and the Canadians in the group in Antarctica. I've spoken to them."

"So you believe I am not a traitor?"

"I believe you, boy. I have to believe, to save the world. So sorry."

Hundreds of miles away, on Mount Tai, Zibb no longer felt Jason near. She searched in her memory for comfort and wasn't so afraid, wasn't so lonely and hungry. She warmed her claws over the fire she had started in the circle of stones with the aid of the pod's small flamethrower.

Queen Taranta was dead.

Zibb was now free.

Chapter Nineteen

Zibb tuned the red box to Jason's bandwidth. The boy had been out of touch for most of the day. Zibb was taking a chance by opening up the airwaves, which the wasps also could hear, but she knew she must be rescued before the wasps found her.

Banter and Bipp, Zibb thought, *You're alive! Oh, my cousins, my dears. I'd given up hope.*

Jason spoke into his ZipPAD. "We're on our way."

Zibb explained how her dear cousins were close. But now the bond with her cousins was broken. She didn't know where exactly they were. She felt more alone than ever, her thoughts and feelings cut off from her kin.

"We're coming to get you," Jason repeated. "The Asian rocket plane did its job, dropped off the food. You didn't eat, did you, Zibb?"

"No. Your plan worked. Queen Taranta is gone. One of the nurses didn't eat. She killed herself when she realized what happened to her monarch. I ate her rations, the ones that were not poison. It kept me alive."

As Zibb was being hoisted by Jason and the Asian soldiers into the megacopter's big cargo area, she heard Banter's voice again. She clutched her red box and thought. *Our telepathic bonds are so fragile. We can't depend on them, and now that our young queen is gone we've lost all sense of unity. We depend now on technology.*

Her red box locked on the last airwave Banter had used. "Explain, Cousin. Where are you?"

"Our pod didn't crash right away like the mother ship and most of the airships. We flew to the south, over low mountains, rice paddies and green fields in the vast middle of China. Then we ran into tall trees while flying low and crashed. Many wasps dead, many more dazed and hurt. We are okay, Cousin."

The Asian megacopter pilot glared at Zibb as she settled from the bucket into the cargo area.

"Where are you? We'll join you, dear Cousins."

"I'll send a map over the scopes. We're in a clearing in a jungle. It's dangerous, injured wasps all around. We'll wait for you, Zibb."

"My little pet and his friends are here."

"Oh."

"They gave us the royal jelly and honeycomb," Zibb explained. "Our queen and her nurses are dead."

"I think I see."

"Yes. It's as you think."

A wasp interrupted the transmission. "Kill the little humans, you wormy slug of a putrid hive."

"Pardon?" Zibb's eye's narrowed.

"Why would the human give you royal jelly?" The wasp snarled into Banter's communicator.

"He's my friend."

"I don't like it. Kill him."

"I've hidden some in the back of the queen's pod here, in the cargo area." Zibb said, changing the subject. "You need it, sir? And the honeycomb? You don't have food in the airship, do you?"

"None of your business, slimy wart-infested fodder. But yes, we need the food and the honeycomb."

"Tell General Vard to come and get it."

"He's monitoring our call from his place in the hills. You can be sure we'll feed our leader first."

The megacopter hung in the air over the jungle, Queen Taranta's body was pulled into the cargo space with the aid of a bucket.

Zibb sent a private message to Jason and told him about the wasp's threats.

"The wasps will share the rest of the royal jelly and honeycomb," Jason said. "I'm sorry, Zibb. We've left the food in the crashed pod where Queen Taranta died, and now you've told the Black Watch where to find it. It's best that way. Please believe me, you've done the right thing."

"What about us? What about Bipp and Banter?"

"We're on our way to rescue them. They mustn't eat the royal jelly and honeycomb we've left either. We'll airlift them out of the jungle first anyhow."

"The food's been changed, pet. Right? You told me not to eat. I didn't eat your poison, little pet. Queen Taranta is dead. The wasps will die. My cousins and I *won't* die. But I was very hungry until I found the nurse's rations. I was so happy to have food." She paused. "Thank you, Jason Anderson."

"Thank you for remembering my name."

The translator whirred, then Jason's voice was gone.

The corners of Zibb's black slit of a mouth turned upward again.

I will survive. And so will my dear Cousins.

The Chinese guards left the bodies of the queen's nurses there, the poisoned royal jelly and honey in the back panel of the pod where the wasps would find them. The pilot locked onto the place Zibb had told them about.

The megacopter used its rocket engines to blast toward the northwest, where in a small valley they found the crashed pod with Banter and Bipp. Dead wasps littered the clearing.

"We're so happy to see you, Cousin," Bipp buzzed. "And I'm so hungry."

"What happened to our queen?" Banter asked.

"It was something she ate," Zibb said.

An Asian guard frowned at the pilot. "What should we throw out, sir, to make room for the aliens?"

The pilot glanced at the clearing, which still burned and smoked with the pieces of the crashed pod. Many dead wasps' bodies lay scattered in the trees. Other wasps crawled through the trees and vines. The first guard fitted a large vial of the tranquilizer into his gun. He aimed at the moving figures seen in the jungle through the infrared lens.

"Don't shoot the worker bees that might be with them," Jason said.

"I can't make out which of them are the wasps," the guard said. "We don't want to hit the friendly bees."

"We're going to make a huge haul," the pilot said. "Like netting fish in the East China Sea. We don't have to throw anything overboard. Only a couple more bees to join us, the rest are like you say in America—bad dudes—and they won't be coming with us."

Jason chewed his fingernails. He knew the Black Watch's strength—*and* their rage.

Will this work?

He wasn't sure.

Zibb fell silent, fearing as well for the safety of her two cousins.

The megacopter rose to tree level and hovered. The figures below stumbled into the jungle then appeared on what seemed to be a path used by water buffalo or elephants. The infrared lenses of the guns could make out the path.

"Dirty rotten insects," mumbled the guard with the scope gun.

"Don't call us insects." Zibb took Jason's hand in her barbed fingers. He seemed surprised but allowed the physical touch to continue.

"Now making a psychic connection." Zibb spoke through the red box. "The poisoned honeycomb was picked up by Black Watch pods. Wasps now dying all over the world. This small troop is cut off from the main body. They are hurt and weak. Soon we'll see the effect of the queen's death."

Zibb reached for Jason's hand again, knowing they were prisoners of the Asians. He seemed to understand and held his friend's furry barbed claws.

You are one of us, Zibb thought.

The bullets held a large amount of Proto-Xybramine, used to put to sleep large animals, and the guard had doubled the dose because the wasps might be resistant to the drug. All held their breath as they saw some wasps drop back and a Black Watch captain stumble and fall. He disappeared from their view.

"Is he dead?" Bipp asked.

Zibb nodded. "I think so."

The pilot brought the large craft as close to the top of the trees as he could. The tractor beam whispered and the large bucket was lowered. The guards used their infrared lenses and their experience with the tractor beam and buckets to guide it. More shots whistled from the guns when the Asian soldiers reached the ground. The wasps sprawled, twisted and dead, in the lush jungle below.

The bucket was raised. Zibb huddled with her cousins in the crowded cargo space of the megacopter as it returned to the Asian base. "I thought you were dead, Bipp."

"No. I won't die," Bipp buzzed.

114

"Me neither. We're going to live, Bipp," Zibb assured her cousin.

"And Queen Taranta ?"

"She ate the royal jelly we left. Enough said," Zibb answered.

"Oh, no." Bipp hung her head and brushed tears of sorrow from her eyes. "Our queen."

"Yes."

"And the other one? The wicked wasp leader?" Banter cracked her claws and trembled.

"General Vard will eat first," Zibb offered. "Enough said about that too, Banter."

"Is that possible?" Bipp asked.

"Your human friends are very smart—and powerful. What happened to our war?" Banter put an arm around Bipp, who whimpered.

"We lost," Zibb said.

"I'm afraid." Bipp held her hands to her eyespots and Banter patted her shoulder.

"We're all afraid," Zibb assured her cousins. "And I'm guilty too. I'm as guilty as my little pet, whom I helped."

"You helped?" Bipp peeked through her black barbed hands.

"We won't talk about it," Banter said

Zibb's slit of a mouth moved upward and she hugged them both.

The megacopter flew northwest toward the Tibet border, where the Asian border soldiers had been told by TelePAD to prepare for their landing.

Aadab called President Maria Black and the scientists in Antarctica.

"We got them," he said. "Queen's dead, serum worked. Alien general will be dead soon and most of the Black Watch gone too. Just a bit of mopping up to do, have to make sure we've wiped out all the wasps and any small killer bees that are left."

"Where are you now?" the President asked.

"We're with the Asian forces on our way to the Tibet-China border. Thanks for your help, Madam President. And please give Jason's father my thanks too. He is a genius. We are very grateful for your American and Canadian science and leadership."

Next Aadab got in touch with the Australians and Americans in New Delhi and arranged to meet them at the Chinese border crossing.

"We have serum," he told them. "We'll share the protein with all your scientists to give out to our leaders right away. Further instructions will come from the Dutch general and his friends in the European Union. We're under their command. See you soon, dudes, in a new paradise on Earth. Allah be praised."

As soon as their allies from New Delhi had taken charge of the dead wasps and the body of their queen, Zibb, Bipp and Banter would fly back to Burma with Jason.

"I'll come with you to Burma. Iodine's already in Burma and found a big house for us. Lots of room for everybody."

"My parents and baby brother are going to meet us there when the war is over, Aadab. War isn't over yet. Still some wasps in mean machines. Next we go to Himachal Pradesh, clean up, take care of business. Go with scope guns and more serum."

"Kill."

"I'm tired of killing, Aadab. But it must be done. No trace of the Black Watch can be left, or they'll hunt us down like ants again."

His ZipPAD showed an incoming call. Captain Lin spoke from his place at the border front. The missiles were quiet. The line was clear.

"Jason?"

"Yes, Captain Lin?"

"The alien general's dead."

"Are you sure?"

"Yes," Lin Ming-Hoa said. "Took the poison and killed him-self with a death ray when he knew he was dying. It's over, my Canadian friend."

Jason could breathe again.

The war was finally over.

Chapter Twenty

The fall of SpaceHive had changed the course of the war. The battle was won, but the final small fights remained. Aadab stared at the scene on the plains in Himachal Pradesh.

Dozens of fiery trails burst in the sky as escape pods burned to Earth. The wasps came out, staggered into the air in short hops, fell twitching to the ground. The Dutch general was in charge, but he spoke often to the Americans in Antarctica. The hotcoms of all nations were busy, and the less-secure PADS Jason and his friends used were electric with voices.

"You're going down in history as the human who ended the war from inside the great skyship, with music and your knowledge of bees and wasps."

"Aadab Ali, you're famous too."

They praised each other even as the UFN killed the rest of the wasps and took the workers and drones to shelter.

"My heart belongs to the world," Jason said. "Well, to the world yes, Aadab, but most of all I'm loyal to my parents, friends and new little brother. My country, Canada, was almost wiped out in the nuclear blasts. Every citizen in the world shares a love for their own country."

"Yeah, Jason. Like me for India."

"This loyalty for one nation and hatred of others divided Earth before the bees and wasps came. Fear of strangers, nationalism, all that divides us must be made right in this new world."

"You saved the world, Jason."

"Each heart must make a choice. Fight together and win, or divide and be conquered." Jason patted his friend on the back. His cotton *kurta* felt smooth and cool. "We fought together and won, Aadab."

Jason's parents waited for him in their house in Burma. Through sheer luck, Burma was untouched by the war. That's where they chose to live then. His father booked Jason on a short trip on a UFN Airship from India to Burma.

He talked to his mother first over his battered ZipPAD, which still worked. Good design, thought Jason. Chinese design, his new friends pointed out.

His father was there too. Jason knew most of his father's story, but he'd only talked to his mother a short time on the patched call that night he reached Antarctica's Station Blue.

"Mom? How'd you survive the radiation?"

"I knew we were safe in the underground bunker in Kamloops. Every day, I'd try my little PAD and talk into the channel I knew you and your father would use. Every day there was no answer."

"You must have been so afraid."

"A little bit, Jason."

"Tell me what happened, Mom. I need to know."

"The bad stuff drifted in from the Purcell and Selkirk mountain ranges near Yahk—the radiation, the burning dust, the night red clouds and winds. The wives and children in our bunker dared not go outside, even after the mother ship left. I waited for your father. I was sure he would rescue us. Your father has always been able to think of ways to get things done. He is reliable and loves us more than his own safety. I knew he'd find us."

"I'd given up, Mom. What did you do while you were waiting?"

"I cataloged the work that was sent to our puter-terminals before we were sealed underground. I found something very interesting with the help of the scientists there—my library information chips and sensors in the bunker. I sent our findings to Antarctica over a special cyber-optic."

"I can guess what they did with it. Dad told me it made it possible for all of you to come out from underground."

His mother nodded. "Japanese and North American physicists discovered a way to stop the radioactivity that covered the continent. They were able to erase its effects completely so it no longer affects living matter."

"That's awesome, Mom."

"Your father, unknown to me, also used our findings in his research to prepare the serum that killed the bees. At the time I couldn't contact anyone by ZipPAD. The awful nuclear winds made sending audio impossible from the bunker."

"It must have been real bad. You didn't know if we were alive or dead."

"I kept the channel open during the day. I'd almost given up hope that you and your father were still alive. I hadn't heard from either of you for many months. I thought you were both...gone."

"I know. The underground bunkers kept you and the baby prisoner."

"Our messages to the outside world didn't get out and nothing got in, so we didn't know anything."

"But we're safe now." *Or at least some of us.*

Jason hugged his mother tightly.

"I love you, Jason," she said, kissing the top of his head.

"Love you too, Mom."

Emily recalled the terror of not knowing if her son and husband were alive. She remembered the moment she first heard Stephen's voice crackling on the other end of the transmission.

"This is KY3 Station Blue. Hello." Then the deep voice so dear to her. "Emily, this is Steve."

"Is it really you? You're alive!" She punched at the ZipPAD and croaked a greeting, voice hoarse with excitement.

Stephen told her of the underground tunnels, the UFN cargo plane, his rescue. The worry, the work, the sleepless nights.

"And Jay?" she asked, holding her breath.

"He disappeared one night. I thought the aliens got him in the forest. But there were rumors of a boy living with the bees."

"So he's alive." Tears pooled in her eyes. "And what about you? Where have you been?"

"The Americans flew me to Antarctica, where I worked with the other scientists. I didn't know if I'd ever see you again. We learned to fix the radioactive clouds and ash—with the help of *your* research."

"My research helped?"

"It was transmitted by cyber-optics to our outpost in Antarctica. I had no way of getting in touch with you because our PAD channel wasn't working."

"It was hard for both of us."

"There was only news now and then on the cyber-optics. I was hoping against hope that you were still alive, the baby was okay and Jason would stay safe."

"We're so lucky, Steve." She let out a sigh. "What about the antidote?"

"It worked, Em. The war is over. We can all go home, start over again." His voice broke and he began to sob. "I can't believe we're all alive."

"I know," she said, wiping her eyes. "I don't understand it. We're so lucky. But the baby…"

"What's wrong with the baby?"

"The doctors say he has radiation sickness." She took a deep breath. "Steve?" Do you think your serum could cure Stephen Jr.?"

"It hasn't been tested on humans. But yes, I believe it can."

"It *must*," she said.

When Jason patched through to Antarctica, to his father and then his mother, he saw at last the despair and how alone he had felt the past eighteen months. Jason had been sure that all was lost that had been dear to him. Then he felt relief and joy. He could go home again and what had happened to him was like a bad dream.

"We left the bunkers as soon as the radiation cloud was neutralized," his mother said. His mother and the baby flew to Burma on a cargo airship with hundreds of others, to be assessed and treated by medical and genetic doctors, to be reunited with her husband and elder son.

"I'm so happy to hear that my robotess teacher and dear old Kitty-Winks are okay. I can hardly wait to see them."

"Sometimes I think you like the robotess and Kitty-Winks more than your parents," his father teased.

The loyal robotess had helped catalog research for his mother, cared for Stephen Jr. and kept the little grey cat alive. By some miracle they survived life in the bunkers.

"I'll follow you, Em and Jason too," his father said. "We'll all be together again. Soon, I promise."

His father had flown eight thousand miles from the Antarctic on a Japanese Thunderbear II to the jungle-covered mountains of South Asia. As a token of appreciation, he was given a beautiful home in Burma, where his wife and baby joined him as soon as he arrived. The meeting was heartfelt and tearful.

"We'll settle here. It's a lovely part of the world," he said. "No radiation or death rays, a little blue-green gem of a place. We can do our research, rest and raise our children here."

It was almost too much to ask of the universe. Jason made the short trip from India to Burma on a small UFN airship. He was tired and his legs ached from the cramped seats, but he grinned when he saw his father waiting for him at the airport.

"It's great to see you, Dad."

"Tell us what happened to you. We want to hear all about it. But first let's meet your mother and brother where they're waiting in our new house. Tomorrow we'll all go to the medical clinic to be checked over. But today we're all together for the first time. My two sons, my wife—my family. It's a miracle. It's over."

His mother didn't leave Jason's side for some time after their greeting. She had to touch him to make sure he was real. "It's almost too much to believe that my son and husband would be returned to me alive."

Jason couldn't stop smiling. With the excitement of the recent events and all his adventures over, he melted into the arms of a plastic recliner in the house in Burma. He welcomed the warmth of home—the sight of his mother's face, the solid body of his father, the softness of his new brother who screamed when he saw him.

"Great kid," Jason said. He stroked the baby's pale chin.

His brother howled some more, his strong little fingers curled around Jason's thumb and he pulled. His face turned red.

Jason grinned.

The newly repaired robotess governess clucked and whirred about on well-oiled wheels, diapers in her silicone hands. Kitty-Winks trailed behind her, a little bit of love.

Stephen Jr. glared at Jason and howled.

"That's my kind of baby."

He pushed himself from the recliner and headed for the greenhouse at the back of the house. He looked out the window at the Anthurium plants blazing in the garden, the room open to the breeze and the yard a wall of color.

He sank onto a cot overlooking the patio. In the distance he heard his brother crying.

He smiled. "My baby brother's got spunk. I like him."

Jason closed his eyes and slept for eighteen hours.

Chapter Twenty-One

Beekeepers came out from underground caves to tame and tend the now passive bees, both big and small. The earth began to blossom and be green once more. Plans were made for the bees to be herded into special areas, protected and helped in their greening of the earth.

Joy filled the lands once again.

"No wasps remain alive," Banter explained to Jason while culling a blossom planted by aliens. "Millions of workers and drones populate far regions of the earth, harmless and dull in the absence of a queen. Many small earth bees survived as well. Plants sown when we first arrived have fruit and blossoms now. It looks like this new and wonderful Jive Hive will support us after all."

"Ironic, isn't it?" Jason said. "You came to destroy us only to find that we can live together in peace. We don't have to kill each other. There is room on Earth for everyone and every life form."

"So... are you ready to go home, Jay?"

"Banter, you're picking up Earth talk." Jason chuckled. "Reminds me of my old friends, Buddy and Grayson." He closed his eyes and swept a lock of hair from his face.

"You never found your two pals again?"

"Haven't found Grayson yet. Presumed killed in the first wave of wasps. Buddy is dead. I saw it happen."

"I'm sorry, pal."

Silence.

Jason was tired. "The Asian Star Shelters move around the countryside, collecting the sick and the healthy, bringing them to new homes far from the ruined lands of North America. Physicians treat those who are sick, like my brother."

"The soil is beginning to mend itself, and our flowers are blooming in the deserts that were scorched by the wasps and their war machines."

"Those who are healthy are reunited right away with their families, if they can be found. I feel surprise and joy. Yes, you could say I'm glad to be home."

While Jason was being examined by a doctor in a room down the hallway. Stephen Sr. waited with Emily and the baby on a plastic bench in the corner. Stephen Jr., it was feared, had developed cancer caused by radiation.

The problem was, the serum that might cure the baby had not yet been tested on a human. It could be dangerous. Fatal even. It needed careful testing, and that would take months.

But there was no time. Stephen Jr. was dying.

"We'll draw lots to see who gets the first injection," one of Stephen's coworkers said.

Stephen Sr. brushed them aside. "I insist I go first. This is *my* son and *my* serum. There's no argument. It has to be me who volunteers. This is my baby's only chance at getting better. Stand aside, lads."

"We don't know what will happen when you inject the serum," a co-worker said. "Too risky. You could die. The world needs you. Choose one of us."

Stephen rolled up his sleeve in the emergency room. "Do it."

Aadab stepped in front of him. "You are married with a family, Stephen. I only have Iodine and she's the love of my life, but I'm still a single man."

"It's not right. I developed the toxin and the antidote, the part of the serum that gives an unlimited lifespan, and I understand the chemistry. It's my duty to test it."

Aadab grabbed the needle.

"No!"

Aadab drew back the plunger and injected the serum into his dusky upper arm. Then he smiled and disposed of the needle in the container nearby. "It's done."

"You fool! It was my place to test the serum. And it could harm you, Aadab. We don't have the same body chemistry as the bees and wasps. We don't know it's safe."

"I know, man. If it don't work, I go join my parents in paradise, is all."

"Stop that!"

Emily moved toward them. "We should go get checked out now, Steve."

He watched as she headed down the hall toward the room where Jason was being examined. Then he turned back to the young Indian man. "You're very brave. And the best friend to my son."

"It's nothing, professor," Aadab said.

They stepped out of the lab into the large admitting area.

Stephen paused. "How do you feel?"

"Like a bee." Aadab chuckled. "Buzzz…" The young man's face turned serious. "You say a prayer to Allah for me, maybe?"

"You won't die. I won't allow it."

They walked down the hall to the examination room. Emily and the baby were being checked out by the doctor, while Jason sat on a chair in the hallway.

"I'll be with you in a minute," one of the nurses said.

Aadab sat in a blue plastic chair in a corner near Jason. "Our alien friends are quiet today," he observed.

"They were dancing in the lobby earlier."

"Nice...uh...aliens."

"Yeah. Without their queen's influence, they're a peaceful bunch."

"What did the army do with General Vard's body?" Aadab asked.

"He's going to be autopsied. Their scientists want to learn more about the wasps. See what makes them so mean and big."

Stephen said nothing as his son and Aadab discussed the general's demise.

"Strangest thing I ever saw," he heard a young doctor say behind him. The man was talking to a group of interns.

"What?" another man asked.

"Well," the doctor said, "they didn't have proper equipment in the bunkers. No test results done there could have been accurate. What do we tell the family?"

Stephen didn't want to eavesdrop so he stumbled to a portal on the wall, inserted a ten-dollar coin and took out a cup of proto-coffee. He sipped it, then returned to his seat across from Jason and Aadab.

"The general was valuable for research," he told Jason and Aadab. "We were lucky to get hold of his body. As we hoped, the bees and wasps fell apart because of his death and the queen's. As far as we know, no wasps remain alive. Without a queen or the general to lead them, they'd be harmless even if they did."

"Now the aliens need a new queen," Aadab said.

Stephen nodded. "Yes. We're thinking we'll give them a new queen. A harmless, quiet queen who'll work with us and rule her subjects peacefully, as I think their old queen did on what they call their old Jive Hive.

"Jive Hive?" Aadab rubbed the sore spot on his upper arm.

"So I understand from Zibb, Bipp and Banter through their translators. The planet they come from used to be a green paradise, dripping with fruit, clear sparkling mountain streams, and honey."

"Sounds ideal. Why'd they leave?"

"Too crowded," Jason said. "Every few hundred years they migrate to another planet after they've used up the resources on the one they live on. They say their species is scattered all over the Milky Way."

Aadab scratched his head. "I also heard talk about deserts and wastelands forming on the old Jive Hive, with workers being forced to live there due to overcrowding. Not good."

"Earth could be the same, if not for the wasp war, which destroyed three quarters of our population," Stephen said. "Before the war, tragic as it was, we faced starvation in many parts of the globe. Too many people. Too many depressed areas where money, food and clean water are sparse. Greedy leaders, natural disasters, civil wars. All of this separation, racism and hatred was all leading to something bad."

"Is there enough food to go around?" Aadab asked.

Stephen shrugged. "We don't know. That was the question here on Earth twenty years ago,"

"Wonder if this is the first time bees and wasps came to Earth." Aadab's forehead wrinkled at the thought.

"Jason's bee friends tell me it's not their first time on Earth," Stephen said. "Their old home is not that far from ours. Their legends say they were driven off by wizards in the mists of time."

"Oh?"

Stephen glanced at his son, who was slumped in his chair, still tired from his long ordeal. *My young lad who saved Earth.*

"Tell me the difference, Aadab, between uber-modern science and magic."

"Sounds like the same thing, to anybody who doesn't know any better. I think maybe Egypt and Atlantis had good science too. The common people thought it was magic. Isn't that what we have now? Magic. No other word for it. We'll be the stuff of future legends, if we all live that long."

Stephen finished his proto-coffee and crushed the cup into a ball. He threw it onto the side of a smooth wall, which opened and swallowed the cup.

Jason opened his eyes and grinned at Aadab. "You sound well enough."

"I'm fine." Aadab rubbed his arm again. "Don't hurt no more."

"We'll give you forty-eight hours to see the effects of the serum and then maybe it can be given to the baby." Stephen frowned and clenched his jaw until a muscle twitched.

"Here comes the doctor, Dad," Jason said, nodding in the direction of a woman in a white jacket.

"What's the story on my family?" Stephen asked her. "Is my wife all right?"

"Her name?"

"Emily Anderson. Stephen Canada Anderson Jr. is our son."

The doctor checked her MediPAD. "Your wife is doing fine. So is your son."

"Wait. My oldest son? Jason?"

"Oh, Jason is fine. A few bruises, scratches. He's very tired and pretty thin. No major problems. We want him to wait out here a bit before going home with you. And the baby is great."

"Great?"

"Yes. No cancer. We checked his blood over and over."

"No cancer?" Stephen fell into a chair beside Aadab. "He's all right?"

"A somewhat rare form of anemia. The lab in the underground bunker wasn't set up to diagnose it right."

"Anemia?"

"He was fine with a D6 and Vitamin B31 shot."

Stephen was so relieved that he could think of no words.

"Go see your family," the doctor said.

"My arm not sore, doctor," Aadab said, indicating a spot on his upper arm.

The doctor smiled. "Phase one of the research study is a success. Congrats, hero." She shut her MediPAD with a snap. "We don't have to check you out, Professor Anderson. You've been given a clean bill of health from Antarctica. All you need is rest."

Stephen nodded. His children were all right. His wife was healthy. He felt well himself.

Emily parted the curtain and came out, the baby in her arms.

"Emily, our family is all right." In a few strides he was beside the two of them. Jason stayed beside Aadab.

"How do you feel, Aadab? Man, I'm so sorry. That wasn't called for after all. You didn't have to do it. The baby's all right."

"Nah, Jason, it had to be done for humanity. We live in a global village now."

The biochemists and physicians ran tests on Aadab, checked his blood work, his urine, his stool, his weight, height, vision, hearing and mental speed. Aadab was going to be okay. The serum wouldn't harm humans. They'd soon know if the Andromeda protein was the immortality drug, the fountain of youth sought for eons by adventurers like Salim Ravid of the late 21st century.

Dreamers, but in this age, impossible dreams came true.

Chapter Twenty-Two

Ten years later.

On the tenth anniversary of the end of the alien invasion, Professor Stephen Anderson, Zibb, Banter, Bipp, Aadab, Iodine, Emily, Jason, and Stephen Jr. were featured in a stereocast of the region's history since the arrival of the Helpers. The robot newscomsters adjusted the controls of the 3-D stereocam, which recorded the scene in Jason's living room in Burma. Green and yellow lights glowed on the 3-D screens.

"That's what they call us now, Bipp. Helpers." Banter crossed two striped legs over another.

"That's not what Steve called us ten years ago."

Banter chuckled that deep bee sound of mirth. "The Helpers. Thank you, newscomsters, on behalf of your network and humanity." Banter clapped Jason on the back. "Congratulations, friend."

"Nice flower tea." Jason sipped from a sturdy mug.

It was a cozy scene, so different from the death and destruction ten years before. His life was almost back to normal—if you didn't count the fact that some of his best friends were giant alien bees.

Jason's father cleared his throat. "The earth has grown lush and green because of alien seeds and plants. Destruction of forests, strip mining, coal mines, uranium mines and oil sands are no longer necessary or put up with."

"Go on," the newscomster said.

"What remained of humanity pulled together since the huge battles which called for a new view of the world as a true global village, no longer divided by language, customs or borders."

"How did this happen?" the newscomster asked as the stereocam whirred.

"The friendship between my son, Jason, and the alien, Zibb, is now documented in history books, and it proves that two alien races can coexist in harmony."

"Do you have any comments on the fate of the alien General Vard and his Black Watch, Professor Anderson?" The newscomster adjusted the sound with deft silicone digits.

Jason's father took a deep breath. "The greedy queen took a lesser place in history than General Vard, who commanded the wasps during the Battle of India. Queen Taranta and General Vard were forced to give in to their own subjects when the Rebellion arrived. The alien queen is dead."

"And Vard?" the newscomster asked.

"General Vard was supported, almost without question, by the Black Watch until his end. He is also dead, his body to be studied for future reference if any of the Black Watch should return."

"But he didn't really die from the poison, did he?"

"No, General Vard did himself in with a death ray. I suppose he knew he was dying anyway and wanting to control even that. There wasn't much left for autopsy, but we're hopeful we'll find some answers to our questions about this alien race. Fortunately, General Vard had brought the queen larvae with him to the earth from the old Jive Hive."

"With it," his father added, "we were able to produce a peaceful queen to lead the bees in this age of harmony and reason."

"You have bees here in your son's home, Professor. We're used to our large friends, of course, but how did this lifetime friendship come about?"

Jason's father crossed his ankles and leaned back in the chair. "The alien known as Zibb adopted Jason as her pet, fed him, helped to release him. The creature loved him. This meant a lot to my son and he loved Zibb in return."

Jason spoke up from his position on the plastic recliner. "I've been loved by a bunch of people including my lovely wife, whom I met here in Burma six years ago. And our daughter, Beatrice." He turned to his daughter. "You want a green Gummigator candy or a blue one, honey?"

Aadab, sitting with Iodine and Jason's father on an orange plastic couch, winked at the small child. "I bet she wants a red one."

"Yes, Daddy, I want a red Gummigator."

Jason's old robotess hummed softly next to Beatrice, and one large LED eye winked.

"You believed you could do it, Jay." His mother poured another cup of tea and inhaled it before sipping. The china cup rang against the saucer when she put it down. "Your father slept on the old beat-up cot in the safety of his underground lab, unable to search for you because the mother ship was sealed. Later his search for Stephen Jr. and me was successful. But we were in agony when we thought you were...gone."

"I know, Mom. Me too."

"Our hope turned to joy when we heard your voice on the PAD shortly after the battle began to turn in our favor."

"I was never in danger, Mom. Not really. I have brains like Dad and a lot of luck. Don't mind telling you, though, I was scared sometimes. Aadab here was a true friend. Zibb too." He looked fondly across the room at Zibb, who was perched on the other orange plastic couch. "You do what you have to do."

His mother nodded. "You were always very good at your studies and you loved all kinds of music, Jay. Your brains saved you. Saved us all. You're a true jack of all trades, a soldier and a scholar. But those long months with the bees in their ship... you must have been lonely."

Jason shrugged.

"Same like me with Iodine," Aadab said. "I missed her so much."

Iodine smiled at him.

"When he was quite young, Jason became an expert of sorts on bee and wasp chemistry, a skill which proved very useful in years to come," his father said. "He was my little shadow in the labs during those early years, but I'm afraid I neglected him in Yahk."

"It changed the world." Aadab adjusted his striped *kurta*.

Jason's father laughed. "We never would've guessed we'd be sitting here ten years later, chatting and drinking tea."

"Where was your family during the war, Mr. Anderson?" a newscomster asked.

"My wife and our unborn child were sent to the underground bunkers near Kamloops with the other families of government workers, while I accepted a government contract and settled in the Kootenay region of southeastern British Columbia with my oldest son Jason."

"And that's when your son met the alien bee."

"Yes. Jason met Zibb the night he strode out onto the road to Cranbrook, with only a light jacket slung over his shoulders, wearing retro sneakers and with his ZipPAD in his pocket."

"That's when my adventure started," Jason said.

Aadab nodded. "Zibb took my Canadian friend to the mother ship. At first a prisoner, later a pet, then a friend and a fellow renegade. Allah be praised."

"We live in a paradise now," Jason's father said. "No bullies. No fights. Food and water for everyone. We all choose our own way in life and anyone can afford a house and any child can have an air scooter. The new serum keeps us all healthy and we may well live forever." He glanced at his wife and tears formed in his eyes.

Jason knew what his father was thinking. His mother was allergic to the serum and would grow old. So his father had chosen not to take the serum, so his hands trembled a bit, he had age spots on his face and his hair was thin.

His mother smiled at his father. "We're very happy."

Stephen Jr. rolled his eyes. He was eleven years old and too young to remember anything of the old world or the war.

Jason was thankful of that.

The robot newscomsters behind the stereocam stopped the recording. The laser neon-green and yellow lights blinked off. They silently rolled out the open door.

"This recording is for the new generations," Aadab said. "For those who have never known life without the friendly aliens. We must learn from our past."

"Many died." Banter's antennae quivered.

"I wish I'd met General Vard," Stephen Jr. said. "I'd have given him *this* and *this*." He made a fist and slammed it into the plastic seat beside him.

Jason shook his head at his young brother. "Vard was not a nice wasp. You are lucky to have never met him."

"General Vard was a very evil alien," Aadab said. "He wouldn't be welcome in the new Jive Hive."

"Right," buzzed Zibb and Bipp together.

"And you wouldn't be so tall if it weren't for the serum in your Go Juice," Banter said. "Remember that, little human Stephen Jr. You're still shorter than we are, and the general was two feet taller than us and very strong."

Jason's gaze flickered from one face to another. Family, friends, even the alien bees. They weren't so alien now. Funny how that worked. First enemies, now friends. And all it took was some understanding and patience.

The world could use more of each.

Chapter Twenty-Three

General Vard opened his eyes. The jungle was ablaze with light. At the far end of the huge arena he saw the young queen Taranta, playing on a field of white flowers, nectar dripping from her jaws, attended by a group of laughing nurses. General Vard rose, whole again, his body aglow with light and energy. All wicked feelings poured like a singing stream away from his mind and spirit.

He strode toward the field of daisies. He knew they were daisies from the new world. He melted into the arms of his beloved queen Taranta. Old queen Selera lay there, too, in the distance, attended by her nurses, whom General Vard remembered from childhood.

It was true, then. This was paradise. No longer did he strut before his Black Watch. The Black Watch looked at him from a distance and they seemed strange, somehow, changed. Hadn't they died in the old world?

General Vard heard a haunting tune from the firesides of his youth. He saw one of his lieutenants put a flute to his mouth and blow. The music! The general began to dance. Queen Taranta whirled in his embrace.

Meteors shot through the sky that night, lighting a path over Burma.

Jason watched the shooting stars until his eyes hurt. Then he went inside to his family. And all was right with the world.

Message from the Author

Dear Reader,

My wish is that you've enjoyed the romp through the beehives of my mind in this, my first published book. It's been fun to write. I would encourage my younger readers especially to make the most of your creativity and follow your dreams. You never know where those dreams will take you!

I started writing poetry when I was five years old and rhymed "stars" with "Mars." I had a dream once about a great treasure. I like to think I've come a long way since then, but maybe I haven't, as the aliens Zibb, Banter and Bipp came from the stars. Jason was transported across the planet and saved the world, our greatest treasure.

Where will your journey take *you*? You're limited only by your imagination.

I like Jason's philosophy: the earth is a global village, inspired by the Canadian philosopher/educator Marshall McLuhan.

~ Kenna

About the Author

Kenna McKinnon is a writer, photographer and self-employed businesswoman, who has lived successfully with schizophrenia for many years. Although her degree is in anthropology (with a minor in psychology), she enjoys exploring the psychology of the human condition, especially when the accompanying human is dropped into complex and unusual circumstances.

Kenna's Young Adult/Middle Grade Sci-fi novel, *SpaceHive*, is her debut novel published by *Imajin Books* in both ebook and trade paperback.

She presently lives in Edmonton, Alberta. She obtained a Bachelor of Arts degree with Distinction from the University of Alberta in 1975. She has two sons, a daughter and three wonderful grandsons.

Lightning Source UK Ltd.
Milton Keynes UK
UKHW020625130121
376872UK00011B/1195/J